No Matter
How Far

ALSO BY BARBARA HINSKE

Available at Amazon in Print, Audio, and for Kindle

The Rosemont Series

Coming to Rosemont

Weaving the Strands

Uncovering Secrets

Drawing Close

Bringing Them Home

Shelving Doubts

Restoring What Was Lost

No Matter How Far

When Dreams There Be

Novellas

The Night Train

The Christmas Club (adapted

for The Hallmark Channel, 2019)

Paws & Pastries

Sweets & Treats

Snowflakes, Cupcakes & Kittens

Workout Wishes & Valentine Kisses

Wishes of Home

Novels in the Guiding Emily Series

Guiding Emily

The Unexpected Path

Over Every Hurdle

Down the Aisle

Novels in the "Who's There?!" Collection

Deadly Parcel

Final Circuit

Connect with BARBARA HINSKE Online

Sign up for her newsletter at **BarbaraHinske.com**
Goodreads.com/BarbaraHinske
Facebook.com/BHinske
Instagram/barbarahinskeauthor
TikTok.com/BarbaraHinske
Pinterest.com/BarbaraHinske
Twitter.com/BarbaraHinske
Search for **Barbara Hinske on YouTub**e
bhinske@gmail.com

NO MATTER HOW FAR

BARBARA HINSKE

CASA DEL NORTHERN PUBLISHING

Copyright © 2021 Barbara Hinske.
  Cover by Elizabeth Mackey, Copyright © 2021.
  All rights reserved.

ISBN: 978-1-7349249-4-7
  Library of Congress Control Number: 2021907182

Casa del Northern Publishing
  Phoenix, Arizona

To my dear friends and genius shopkeepers Helen Burland and Pepper Rusnak. You are examples of how to live an accomplished, gracious, and generous life, and the inspiration for Judy Young and Celebrations in my Rosemont series.

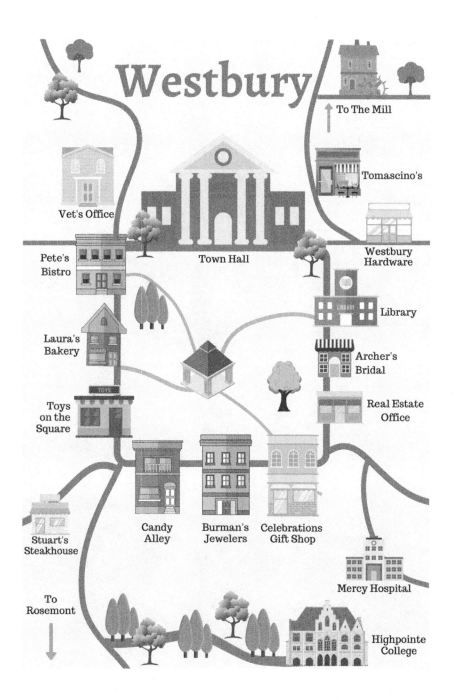

Westbury

↑ To The Mill

Tomascino's

Vet's Office

Town Hall

Westbury
Hardware

Pete's
Bistro

Library

Laura's
Bakery

Archer's
Bridal

Toys
on the
Square

Real Estate
Office

Stuart's
Steakhouse

Candy
Alley

Burman's
Jewelers

Celebrations
Gift Shop

Mercy Hospital

To
Rosemont
↓

Highpointe
College

PROLOGUE

*J*udy Jorgensen turned into the alley and picked her way carefully across the rutted snow, packed with gravel and bits of broken twigs. A fall on this terrain was sure to tear a hole in her tights. An icy wind blew under her skirt and bit through the thick Fair Isle scarf that her mother had made her last Christmas. She should have listened to her mother and worn the snow pants, but at twelve, she felt too old for unfashionable practicalities.

One mittened hand tucked a loose strand of her waist-length dark hair into her collar as she ran the other along the smooth stones of the wall that bracketed the alley. She leaned forward, keeping her eyes on her footing. She knew every inch of the passage from the school to the back gate of her mother's shop.

Celebrations, located on Westbury's town square, had been the community's source for stationery, gifts, and invitations since her grandmother had founded the business decades ago. When school was over, a snack would be waiting for her, along with the back inventory she'd have to help her mother stock. Judy kicked a rock down the alley. It landed in front of the wrought-iron gate that sat across the alley from Celebrations.

The street behind the shops on the town square was lined with charming historic homes, including the one that Judy and her mother had inherited from her grandmother. The residence on the other side of the iron gate was the grandest of them all. The towering, three-story Victorian—built by the first president of Highpointe College—was now home to the man's reclusive great-grandson.

Uncharitable rumors swirled around town about the elderly man, but William Olsson had never been anything but kind to Judy and her mother.

"He's just a private soul," her mother would say whenever she heard one of these rumors. "He's never hurt anyone. And he keeps me in business! His house and that beautiful garden of his bring in tourists every year!"

After church, Judy's mother would wrap up a serving of Sunday dinner and hand it to her. "Leave it in the stone wall's alcove next to the iron gate." She said it *every* time—even though Judy had been doing this for what felt to her like her entire life.

The next day, William would leave something from his gardens in the alcove for Judy and her mother. In spring, Judy would find fresh-cut flowers tied up with twine. Summer brought hydrangeas, fresh herbs, and strawberries. In fall, there'd be apples, chrysanthemums, pansies, and, as it grew colder, root vegetables and exotic hothouse blooms. But today, like every Monday before Christmas, Judy would find the best gift of all.

She stopped to claw at the hair the wind held plastered to

her face and stepped closer to the nook and released the breath she'd been holding.

It was there. In the alcove.

She reached up and removed the package wrapped in tissue and tied with a thin red ribbon. She tucked it inside her coat and turned toward her gate.

She hoped that her mother wouldn't be busy with customers. They always unwrapped his gift together. She didn't want to wait.

CHAPTER 1

*J*udy Young stepped onto the sidewalk and inhaled deeply. The scent of apple blossom hung heavy on this spring morning. The tree in her front yard was thick with pink and white blooms. She'd have a bumper crop of Pink Ladies in the fall—enough to make pies for the church bake sale and to can for applesauce.

She set out for her shop at a quick pace. Walking the short distance to Celebrations when the weather was fine was one of her favorite things, especially since she could look at her neighbors' homes as she passed by. She recognized every plant in the well-tended gardens and knew which shutters had just received a fresh coat of paint or which porch swing needed repair. She'd lived on this street for more than forty years, inheriting the family home and the shop when her mother had died.

Judy clipped along, avoiding familiar cracks where roots of the now-mature trees lifted the pavement, until she came to the Olsson house. The old Victorian home rose three stories, towering over its neighbors.

She squinted and tilted her head upward, inspecting the gabled roof and the windows that circled the turret. Each time she passed, Judy noticed small changes and grieved the home's steady decline. After William Olsson's death in the early 1990s, the house was left vacant but well maintained—until four years ago. She was running her eyes over the façade when she spotted a white piece of paper with the word "NOTICE" in heavy black type affixed to the front door. She'd have to get closer to read the words that followed.

Judy looked at her watch. She really shouldn't dally—the delivery service would soon be at the back door of Celebrations with her weekly shipment of cards and stationery.

She pushed against the wrought-iron gate that hung crookedly on its rusty hinges. It screeched open a mere twelve inches before it caught on a high spot on the sidewalk. Judy squeezed herself through the opening and picked her way carefully through the weeds and brambles that had taken over the once manicured lawn. A branch caught at her cardigan, and she pulled it away, tearing a small hole in her sleeve.

"Darn it," she muttered. She mounted the stone steps to the double front door and leaned in to read the piece of paper that was stapled there.

Judy gasped. The Olsson house was going to be auctioned off for back taxes. What did that mean? Her stomach lurched, and for a moment, she worried that she might be sick. Judy had never been inside the house, but it had been a special part of her life. Every Christmas, her mother and Mr. Olsson had exchanged gifts through the alcove in the alley. This notice felt like a leech on the house—a violation of her past. She grasped the offending paper and began to tug but stopped herself. Pulling it down wouldn't accomplish anything—and was illegal. It said so on the notice.

She took several deep breaths to steady herself, then snapped a photo of the offending notice with her phone. She'd text the photo to Susan Scanlon. Her young friend was a brilliant lawyer and could explain what this tax sale meant.

"You're sure I'm all set to bid?" Judy curled the papers she was holding into a tight cylinder and tapped it against her leg.

The tall, blonde woman in her tailored blue suit, crisp white blouse, and high-heeled pumps turned to her friend. "You're qualified. We've filed all of the required paperwork and financial assurances." Susan smiled encouragingly at Judy.

"Okay. Good." Judy shifted her weight from foot to foot.

A man approached a podium set up on the courthouse steps and tapped on a microphone, sending sharp crackling sounds into the air. The sunny spring morning was cool, and a light breeze ruffled the papers he set onto the podium. "Ladies and gentlemen, we're here for this afternoon's tax auction. If you've prequalified to bid, you'll have a number on a sheet of paper. Hold it up, and we'll take your bid. Our first address is …"

"How many did you say are ahead of us?" Judy asked.

Susan consulted her copy of the papers that Judy clutched in her hand. "Six. We shouldn't have long to wait."

"What happens if nobody bids?"

"The unpaid taxes continue to pile up," Susan said.

Judy nodded. "Do you think I'm the only bidder for the Olsson house?"

Susan looked at the others around them. "I recognize one of the bidders. He's a real estate developer. I suspect he's here to bid on the Olsson house. It's a double lot—prime property. He could tear the house down and put up eight patio homes without having to rezone it."

Judy groaned. "That would be a travesty—like trading the family silver for plastic cutlery."

Susan put a protective arm around Judy's shoulder. She loved all of her mother's close friends but felt a particular affinity for Judy. "Why don't you watch these other auctions—get a feel for how they go. It'll be your turn soon enough."

Judy inhaled sharply and nodded.

As the auctioneer droned on, she wrung the papers in her hands, rolling them tighter and tighter. When they finally announced the sale she was interested in, the papers fell to her side and she stepped forward.

"You've got this," Susan said. "Remember, the first bid has to be for the full amount of the back taxes." She handed Judy a three-by-five card where she'd printed the correct amount.

Judy nodded, raised her number, and made the required bid.

The auctioneer repeated the amount and asked for additional bids.

Judy focused on the real estate developer and held her breath.

The man raised his number and added a thousand dollars to Judy's bid.

Judy thrust her number in the air and added another thousand dollars.

She and the developer continued, raising each other by a thousand dollars each time for the next five minutes.

Susan leaned close to Judy's ear. "You're now at the maximum bid that you decided on before we got here."

The developer added another thousand, and so did Judy.

"It's easy to get carried away in an auction," Susan said.

"I can't let that bastard tear it down and turn the place into … God knows what."

"We don't know what he plans to do with it."

The developer increased his bid by two thousand.

"So that's how he intends to get the better of me." Judy's face grew red.

"Don't let your emotions take over!"

Judy raised her number and yelled, "Ten thousand more!"

Susan swung to her friend and client, who looked as surprised by her most recent bid as Susan did.

They both turned to the developer. He crumpled the paper with his number on it and turned to smirk at Judy. "Lady, you have no idea what you just stepped in. When you're done throwing your money into the financial abyss, give me a call."

The auctioneer gaveled the sale, announcing that that was the last item on the day's agenda. The crowd of bidders began to disperse.

Judy reached out a hand and grabbed Susan's arm to steady herself. "What in the hell did I just do?"

"You bought yourself that gorgeous Olsson house. Congratulations."

"I spent *way* more than I intended to. I don't want to even think about how much."

"You got an incredible property at a remarkably good price."

"You tried to stop me." Judy sounded close to tears. "Why didn't I listen to you? The place is a wreck—it'll be a complete money pit."

"Stop it," Susan said firmly. "You were going on your gut instinct. Don't second-guess yourself now. Enjoy this moment —you got what you came here for."

"I don't really own it for another six months, right?"

"Yes. Parties in interest can redeem the taxes and retain ownership."

Judy's breathing was coming in fits and starts. "So, I may not ever own it—the real owners could still come forward?"

"It's possible." Susan took Judy by the shoulders and turned her toward her. "I don't think that's likely. If the real owners were interested, they wouldn't have let the property go to tax sale."

Judy moaned. "I can't believe I just did this."

"Listen to me." Susan's tone was firm. "Pay the auctioneer and then forget all about this for the next six months. There's nothing you can do about it now. When you get the deed, you'll go through the property, assess its condition, and decide what to do with it. If it's too big a job to tackle, you can put it on the market. I'll bet you'll get an offer from that developer the moment you list it."

Judy swallowed hard. "That's comforting. I'd have a tough time selling to anyone who wanted to tear it down, but at least I have a few ways out of this mess."

"You do. And stop thinking of it as a mess! Buying this house might be the key to something unexpected and wonderful."

Judy grinned. "You're just like your mother, with all of that hopefulness. That's why I love both you and Maggie!"

CHAPTER 2

*J*eff Carson drained the last of the coffee from his cup, rinsed it, and placed it in the strainer by the sink—as he had done every morning for more than thirty years. For the past three years, there had only been one cup by the sink. Losing Millie had been devastating, but he'd finally come to terms with her death.

The horizon was just beginning to shift from black to gray, streaked with swaths of pink and gold. He'd always been an early riser, and today would be no exception. The routine he'd followed—that had kept him grounded during Millie's drawn-out battle with cancer—would soon no longer be part of his life. Today would mark a sea change.

He forced himself to turn away from the window. Jeff found his warm jacket—his "back door" jacket as Millie had called it—and went out to the garage. His son and daughter-in-law would be there any minute to help with the sale. He was getting rid of the accumulated trappings of a life that, against his every hope and prayer, was no longer his to live. It was high time to forge a new path for himself. In his early sixties and in good health, he still had a lot to offer this world. Millie would be cross at him for taking so long to rechart his path.

He crossed the back porch, listening to the squeak at the top step that he'd never been able to fix, and went to the garage. He opened the door and turned on the overhead light, surveying the tables jammed into the stall that usually held his car. Boxes, bins, and totes brimming with things priced to sell—the bits and pieces of his life in this place—were everywhere.

His daughter-in-law had worked hard, pricing every item and grouping them "to maximize sales." Sharon had even advertised in the small community newspaper, and she and Jason were putting up sales signs on their way over. She said they'd make a killing. Jeff said nothing, but he thought the whole thing was more trouble than it was worth and wanted to donate the lot of it. Now, looking over what Sharon had pulled off, he had to admit she might be right and that made him happy because he planned to donate all of the proceeds to the animal shelter.

Millie had first met Sharon at the shelter. Millie had been a volunteer and Sharon worked there, as a teenager, cleaning out cages. Millie befriended the hardworking teen and introduced her to Jason. The rest, as they say, was history. Jeff knew that Sharon would be thrilled to have the money donated to the shelter in Millie's memory.

Jeff checked his watch. It was getting close to opening, and cars were starting to line along the curb. Where were Jason and Sharon? Part of the deal was that he wouldn't have to talk to the shoppers, haggling over the pieces of his former life.

He dragged a table onto the driveway and went back for another. He was inching the heavily laden table forward when one of the legs hit a crack in the concrete. The jolt sent a small cardboard box tumbling over the edge.

He picked it up and froze when he glanced at the contents. There, nestled in white tissue paper, lay an intricate three-dimensional wooden snowflake. In today's world, such an object would be laser cut by a machine. This was handcrafted.

He recognized this ornament. It had been part of his childhood—a treasure he hadn't seen in decades. His uncle, William Olsson, had hand-carved it for Jeff's mother. Alma had received the gift while she and her brother were still on speaking terms —long before her mental illness drove her to hostility, hoarding, and isolation.

Jeff remembered the Christmas his uncle William had arrived from Sweden to give his mother the exquisite ornament. Even as a child, he'd been mesmerized by its complexity; it looked different from every angle.

Jeff leaned on the table, both of his arms stiff. He hadn't thought about this treasure from his childhood in years. When his mother died four years ago, Millie's health was declining, and Jeff didn't have the time or energy to deal with any of it. His mother's things were boxed up and sent to him after her death, and he'd never gone through them. Now here they sat; Sharon had simply added their contents to the garage sale.

Seeing this tie to his past brought a surge of longing and regret. He wished—not for the first time—that he'd been able to break through his mother's mental illness and form a bridge across their hurt and estrangement. At the time of her death, he hadn't seen or talked to her for over twenty years.

He remained hunched over the table until headlights swung across the driveway and Jason's car pulled to the curb.

He straightened and rubbed a hand over his eyes. Jeff began to replace the box on the table and then stopped. This ornament was the only physical link he had to his mother and his uncle—and to one of the only happy memories of his childhood.

Jeff waved to his son as he was getting out of his car. "Be right back," Jeff called as he sprinted up the steps to his back door and placed the box with the ornament on the kitchen table. Wherever he wound up in his new life, he would bring this keepsake with him.

CHAPTER 3

aggie Martin circled the block, looking for a parking space. The shops along the town square were busy on this late afternoon in early November. After several late nights, she'd finished the draft of her "Report of the President" for the Highpointe College trustees and decided she deserved to leave the office a few hours early. She'd pick up a gift at Celebrations for the Spanish department head who was retiring after thirty-eight years of service and then head home to Rosemont. She might even surprise her husband, John Allen, DVM, with a home-cooked meal on a weeknight.

Maggie approached the shop and was stunned to see the Closed sign in the window. She'd never known Judy to close early. She hoped everything was okay with her friend. She'd have to call or text her after dinner to find out.

Maggie turned the corner onto the street that ran behind the town square. She often drove this way, admiring the charming, historic homes that sat back from the curb at the end of deep lawns. Although it was in serious decline, her favorite was the old Olsson house.

Maggie drove toward the house and was surprised to see two cars and a pickup parked in front. The lettering on the side of the truck proclaimed that the owner was Westbury's Best Locksmith. Two women stood on the sidewalk, talking and pointing to the house. Maggie's eyes widened—her daughter was one of them. What was Susan doing, loitering on a curb in the middle of the afternoon with Judy?

A man got out of the pickup. He opened the gate and pushed his way through the overgrowth of weeds to the front door.

Maggie parallel parked in front of the truck and waved to them as she got out of the car.

"Hey," Maggie said.

Judy and Susan spun to face her.

"Hi, Mom." Susan took a step back, moving so that Maggie could join them.

"What're you two up to?" Maggie looked at her daughter and then her friend. "I've never known you to close Celebrations early. I was worried something might be wrong."

Susan glanced nervously over her shoulder to Judy.

"We ... I ..." Judy stammered and quickly looked away. "I bought the old Olsson place," she said, pointing to the house.

Maggie brought her hand to her chest. "I didn't know it was on the market."

"It wasn't," Judy said. "Not exactly." She swiveled to Susan. "Can you explain?"

"Judy bought the back taxes on the property. The redemption period has expired, and she's now the legal owner. I just brought her the treasurer's deed."

"Wait a minute," Maggie said. "What?"

"I'll explain it all later. Right now, the locksmith is rekeying the place. Judy's about to get her first glimpse inside."

"You mean to tell me you bought the place and you haven't been inside it?" Maggie turned her collar up against the chilly air.

Judy nodded again and gestured to Susan.

"That's how a tax sale works," Susan said. "You don't get to do an inspection or any due diligence."

"I had no idea," Maggie said. "I guess you got it pretty cheap."

Judy nodded.

"What in the world are you going to do with it? Will you sell your place and move down the block to this house?"

"No way," Judy said. "I love my house. I'd never move."

"That's what I thought," Maggie replied. "Then why did you buy it?"

"To tell you the honest truth," Judy said, "I have no idea. I've lived down the street from the place my entire life. My mother and I once knew—well, sort of knew—the old man who lived there. I've always been fascinated by it."

"Who wouldn't be?" Maggie said. "It must have been magnificent, back in the day. Before it was abandoned."

"It was. William died more than two decades ago, but someone maintained it and paid the taxes. It was such a mystery—no one ever moved in after his death or even visited the place. Then, four years ago, everything abruptly changed. The house and grounds went to seed. I found the tax sale notice posted on the front door this spring and called Susan. We went to the sale and, well, here we are."

"That still doesn't explain why you wanted it."

"I'm still trying to figure that out for myself. I was convinced that someone would redeem the taxes, and I'd get my money back, plus interest. Until Susan called to tell me that the treasurer's deed had gone through, I didn't really believe I'd end up owning it."

"Why didn't you tell me?"

"I thought it was a completely crazy thing to do in the first place. And I didn't think it would ever really be mine. I guess I didn't want to look foolish."

Maggie put her arm around her friend's shoulder and looked up at the fine example of Victorian architecture. "Doing things for the love of a house is never crazy. Not to me."

Judy leaned into her friend. "I should have known you'd understand."

A familiar pickup truck pulled to the curb on the opposite side of the street. Sam and Joan Torres got out. They both held flashlights. Joan hurried over to the three women while Sam rummaged in the back of his truck and produced three more flashlights. He joined them.

"The power's not on," Sam said, handing each of them a flashlight. "The utility departments will want to check the place before they reconnect water, gas, or electricity. I won't be able to do a thorough inspection until they're back on, either, but I knew you were dying to have a good look at this place."

"Thank you, Sam," Judy said. "I'm so glad you're here. I'm hoping you can get an idea of how much work the place needs once we get in there."

"I'll do my best," said everyone's favorite handyman.

"I hope you don't mind that I came, too," Joan said. "I'm beyond curious about this place."

"Not at all." Judy squeezed her friend's arm. "I'm glad you're here."

The four women moved along the path to join the locksmith, now bent to his task.

"Would you look at all of this carved wooden trim on the

porch banister and around the transom above the door," Susan said. "The paint's all chipped off, but it reminds me of those Painted Ladies that San Francisco is so famous for."

"When I was a child, all this trim detail was meticulously painted." Judy bent to examine a column. "Some of the wood has rotted out. I shudder to think what it'll cost to restore all this." She pressed her fingers into her lips. "I must have been out of my mind to buy this place."

"None of that." Maggie touched Judy's elbow. "There's no point in imagining the worst when you don't know the facts." She tilted her head back and swept her arm in an arc across the house. "Just look at this magnificent place. How in the world could you *not* have bought it?"

"You really think so? Would you have done the same thing?"

"In a heartbeat," Maggie said.

The door creaked as it swung open on its hinges, announcing that the locksmith had accomplished his mission. The group on the porch parted, and the locksmith motioned for Judy to enter her new house.

CHAPTER 4

The sun, hidden behind thick clouds all afternoon, escaped its confinement, and its rays suddenly flooded the foyer through the open door. Judy stepped onto the parquet floor and stood motionless, drinking in the scene in front of her.

A wooden staircase, with an intricately carved banister, hugged the inside of the turret. It rose ten feet before halting in a wide landing illuminated in blues, oranges, and yellows as the sun streamed through a large stained-glass window. The stairway then turned to rise again, disappearing out of sight.

Susan, Maggie, and Joan waited behind her, wishing she would move inside so they could see what held her raptured attention.

"Oh … my … gosh," she gushed as she crossed over the threshold.

Sam followed the four women into the foyer.

"Look at this!" Joan said, heading for the staircase.

"Let's not go up there," Sam said, rushing over to her. He

bent to have a closer look at it. "We don't know if it's structurally sound." He lifted his head to find four pairs of eyes staring at him with expressions ranging from skepticism to hostility. These women wanted to go upstairs.

"Look at this carpet," he said, pointing to the shreds of a once-red carpet on the treads. "It's in terrible shape."

Their expressions didn't change.

"Do you have to go upstairs today?"

They all nodded.

"I'll tell you what. Why don't you look around the first floor and let me determine if the stairs are safe?"

"We can do that," Judy said.

French doors led off of both sides of the generous foyer. The doors on the left opened to what must have once been a magnificently furnished parlor. Heavy velvet drapes, now torn and sagging, lined floor-to-ceiling windows. Upholstered chairs and settees with heavily carved arms filled the room, where a large fireplace with an impressive mantel dominated the space.

Susan moved to a chair and ottoman that were pulled up to the fireplace, now cold and full of ashes. A pipe on a ceramic dish rested on a small round pedestal table next to the chair, and a newspaper lay on the floor nearby. She picked it up and read the date.

"This paper is from the day William Olsson passed," she said. "It says he died at home. Of natural causes."

"Gosh," Judy said, taking the paper from Susan and then putting it down carefully. "I wonder if anyone's been in here since then."

"It feels almost like seeing a room in a museum—like we're on the other side of a red rope," Joan said.

They crossed the foyer and entered a room furnished with a

grand piano and settees that ran along the walls. The remainder of the first floor contained an elaborate dining room, a morning room, a tiny powder room that had likely been added in the twentieth century, and the kitchen.

"I feel like I've stepped back in time," Judy said. "These appliances look like they're from the fifties." She rubbed her hands together. "What have I gotten myself into? This entire kitchen needs to be gutted. I think I've bought myself the biggest money pit of all time."

A coffee cup sat upended on a drainboard, and a breadbox gaped open on the counter, a trail of mouse droppings leading from it to the sink.

"Oh my gosh," Judy said, peering at the scat. "I've got a rodent infestation!"

"All of this can easily be cleaned up," Joan said, putting her hand on Judy's back as she surveyed the scene in front of her.

A small kitchen table stood in the middle of the room. A straight-backed wooden chair lay on its side by the table, with a book and a pair of shattered reading glasses strewn across the floor.

"It feels like we're walking in on someone who's just left," Judy said. Her voice quavered. "I don't know if I like this. I feel like we're intruding."

"I find it sort of comforting," Maggie said. "We know that William took great care of his garden. It's clear that he maintained the house, too." She raised her hand to point behind her. "This house must have been magnificent in the day. Surely he wouldn't have wanted it to fall into its current state of disrepair. I'll bet that he's looking down on you, Judy—*right now*—and saying, 'Thank God that little girl bought my house!'"

Judy laughed. "You think so?"

"Absolutely," Maggie said.

"Mom's right," Susan said. "I don't want to sound kooky, but there's a warm, welcoming feel to this place."

"I agree with you both," Joan said. "The house is happy with you, Judy. I can sense it, just like I did when Maggie took over Rosemont."

"Rosemont had been vacant for quite a while when I inherited it," Maggie said. "The idea of restoring a mansion was daunting, at first, but once we started in on it, the project wasn't so bad. Sam did all the hard stuff, of course." She smiled at Joan. "Thank God for that husband of yours. I just had the fun of decorating it."

"Rosemont's an even bigger house than this one, and you got it whipped into shape. It's beautiful, now." Judy looked at Maggie. "You really think I can do this? Without going broke?"

"You'll know more when Sam's finished his inspection, but I think the answer to that is going to be a resounding yes."

Judy smiled at her friends. "You're the best, you know that? Now—let's go see if that killjoy husband of Joan's is going to let us go upstairs."

SAM WAS HEADED to the kitchen when the four women found him. "Done exploring for the day?" he asked. "The sun will be setting any minute now, and we'll be completely in the dark."

"We've got plenty of light from these flashlights of yours," Judy said. "Are the stairs safe?"

"Yes. I've checked them out. The interior appears to be in reasonably decent shape. I couldn't really see in this light, of course, but I don't see any signs of water damage or ..."

Judy held up a hand to stop him. "I'm looking forward to

getting your full inspection report," she said. "But for now, we just want to take a quick look upstairs."

After almost fifty years of marriage to Joan, Sam knew when to give in to a woman on a mission. "Go ahead. I'll check out the electrical panel outside."

"Thank you!"

"I'll let you know when I'm done," Sam said. "I shouldn't be more than ten minutes."

"Perfect," Judy called as she followed the others, already on their way up the stairs to the second floor.

Their inspection disclosed six bedrooms, each with a fireplace and an attached bathroom. Carved canopy beds dominated each room. The drapes and bed linens were deteriorating with age, and a thick coating of dust covered every surface, looking like an undisturbed blanket of fresh snow.

"Gosh," Maggie sighed wistfully. "Are you sure you don't want to move in here—when it's all cleaned up?"

"It's magnificent, all right," Joan agreed.

"What's that at the end of the hall?" Susan ran her flashlight over a small, plain door that sat partially open.

"That's the stairs to the turret room," Sam replied, coming down the hall to join them.

The women turned to him.

"Those windows circling the turret are in a small room at the top of those stairs," he said. "There's another door in that room that I think goes to the attic. I didn't take the time to find out."

"So, these stairs are safe, too?" Judy asked.

"Well … yes … but not tonight. It's too dark to go up there with just your flashlight." He turned to his wife. "We've got choir practice tonight, remember? We've got to go. We'll be late, as it is."

Susan shone the flashlight on her watch. "I've got to run, too. I have to pick up Julia from the babysitter. That toddler is an absolute bear to put to bed if her routine gets off."

The group began to move to the stairs.

"Give my granddaughter a hug and kiss from me," Maggie said. "Tell her that her grandpa and I can't wait to keep her overnight on Friday. We're so excited."

"Believe me," Susan said. "Nobody's looking forward to Friday more than Aaron and me. It's been months since we've slept in."

They arrived at the front door, and Susan, Sam, and Joan stepped onto the porch. Judy and Maggie remained inside.

"The yard and garden are seriously overgrown, but I think you'll be able to save most of the foundation plantings. You'll need to have someone come in and cut all of this down so you can see what you have," Sam said.

"I'll get a hold of Joe Appleby tomorrow," Judy said. "I'm hoping to restore the path through the backyard to the gate. I'd like to be able to nip over here from Celebrations through the alley."

"That should be possible," Sam said. He looked up at the house. "You may feel like you've got a tiger by the tail, but you're going to have a magnificent home when you're done making it livable again." He winked at Maggie. "Second only to Rosemont."

"My head's spinning. I woke up feeling I'd made the dumbest decision of my life when I bought this place." Her voice quivered. "I'm still not so sure. All I can see is stuff that needs to be done and dollars flying out of my bank account."

"I think you've made the real estate deal of the decade," Susan said. "Don't get cold feet now. Be proud of yourself." She clicked off her flashlight and handed it to Sam. "This was so much fun. Have a good evening, everybody." She turned to face Judy. "Call me if you have any questions about your deed."

Sam turned back to Judy and Maggie. "Surely you're not planning to keep looking around by flashlight?"

Judy shrugged.

"Why don't you wait until the electricity is back on?"

"When will that be?"

"You'll have to replace your electrical panel first. It's not up to code."

"Can you do that for me?"

"I'll contact an electrician I work with," he said. "It'll be expensive."

"How much?"

"I'm guessing six or seven thousand."

Judy swallowed hard. As she'd feared, the money was about to start flowing out. "Will you get him started?"

"I'll text him tonight."

"How long will it take?"

"I'll let you know. If he can come out this week, you might be able to have the power turned on by the end of next week."

"Okay. Fine," Judy said. She and Maggie exchanged a glance. "You go along. I'm not going to be responsible for your being late to choir practice." She smiled sweetly. "We'll lock up and be right behind you."

"WE'RE NOT LEAVING RIGHT NOW, ARE we?" Maggie asked as Judy shut the door.

"No way am I going to wait until the end of next week to see that turret room."

"You could come back tomorrow, during the daytime,"

Maggie suggested as the two women turned on their flashlights and illuminated their path up the stairs and to the end of the hallway on the second floor.

"Or you and I could take a quick look at the turret room and the attic beyond." Judy chuckled gleefully. "I have a turret room. Can you imagine?"

"That's pretty cool," Maggie agreed. She swung her flashlight in a circle around her.

"Why are you doing that?"

"I'm looking for something to prop this door open. I don't fancy getting trapped in a dusty attic again."

"That's right! You got stranded in the Rosemont attic for hours."

"I'd given up hope anyone would come looking for me that late in the afternoon. I was tying sheets into a makeshift three-story ladder to climb down. I was scared witless that I'd lose my grip and fall to my death."

"How could I have forgotten that?"

"Thanks to Frank Haynes, it turned out all right, but it was terrifying at the time." She began searching for something to use as a doorstop.

"I guess I only remember the good part—all the cool treasures you found up there. I hope I'm as lucky."

Maggie's light illuminated a tall urn on top of a dresser in the hallway. She walked over to it and hoisted it into her arms.

"This thing weighs a ton," she said. "It'll keep the door open." She squatted and positioned it against the open door to the stairs leading to the third floor.

"Let's go," Judy said, training her light in front of her and leading the way.

The turret room sat at the top of the narrow flight of stairs. Leaded glass windows ringed three sides of the room, casting a faint silver glow on this cloudy night. The room sat empty except for a circular wrought-iron bench.

Judy brushed the dust from a portion of the bench and sat. "The trees in the front yard are blocking the view now, but I bet it'll be spectacular when I get them trimmed."

Maggie stepped to the window. "I think you're right. You'll be able to see the Highpointe Library steeple from here."

"I'm starting to get cold," Judy said, rising. "Let's take a quick peek inside the attic. My imagination is racing after all of this talk of Rosemont's attic. I want to know if it's vacant or full of stuff that might yield treasures."

"I'm glad you said that," Maggie said. "I'm curious, too."

Judy seized the round door handle and turned it. The door wasn't locked. It started to give and then caught on something. Judy tugged and pulled to no avail. "Darn it. Looks like we'll have to wait until Sam comes back."

"Stand back," Maggie said. She tapped along the edge of the door with her fist. "I learned this trick from him. Almost all of the doors at Rosemont stick from time to time. Now try it."

Judy turned the handle, and the door swung open.

The beam from Maggie's flashlight punctured the space with light. A small, furry form skittered into the dark recesses of the attic.

"Eek!" Judy shrieked. "I've got rodents, top to bottom."

Maggie traced trunks and boxes stacked to the ceiling. A dress form lay, tipped on its side at an indecent angle, across a low table. Fishing rods, snowshoes, and tennis rackets leaned against the wall.

Judy switched on her flashlight and trained it on the rafters. "I wonder if there're bats in here?" She shivered involuntarily.

"I didn't even think of that," Maggie replied. "I hope not."

They stood in the doorway, unwilling to explore what lay before them without anything other than their flashlight beams.

"You're going to find some incredible things in here," Maggie finally said.

"I hope you're right. It's fun to know all this is up here, but I'm not going any further until I've had the exterminator up here."

"That's a wise plan."

"When I can get up here, do you want to be with me? I know how busy you are and everything," Judy hastened to add.

"I think you know me well enough to know the answer to that question," Maggie said. "Just tell me when and I'll be here."

"Sunday afternoon?" Judy replied. "I should be able to get an exterminator out here by the end of the week. This is going to be so much fun!"

Maggie pulled her coat close around herself, and they moved to the front door, which Judy closed and locked with the new key the locksmith had given her. "I won't be able to sleep tonight, wondering about what might be in the attic."

"I have to admit, my mind is going a mile a minute, thinking of the possibilities."

They headed for their cars, each one fantasizing about the secrets hidden in the old house.

CHAPTER 5

*J*eff approached the tiny office at the back of the hardware store. Jason would be tallying the day's receipts and getting the deposit ready for the night drop at the bank. Jeff had done the same when he'd owned the store. Now that he'd sold his interest to his son, this job fell to Jason.

He looked up from his desk when he heard his father's footsteps. "What're you still doing here? The store's been closed for an hour."

"I was tinkering with the display of rakes and wheelbarrows," Jeff said. "People are getting their yards and gardens ready for winter. It's time to mulch roses—before it snows. I added bags of mulch and pruning shears."

"You're always thinking about the business, aren't you?"

Jeff smiled at his son. "I guess old habits die hard. Does that bother you? The business is yours, now. You should be calling all the shots without interference from the prior owner."

"Not at all, Dad. I learned everything I know from you, and I appreciate your help. I'm glad you decided to stay on."

Jeff turned his head quickly aside. "Why don't you get on home? You'll be in time for dinner, and you can help the kids with their homework before they go to bed. I'll run the deposit to the bank."

"Then you'll be late for dinner."

"I already told Sharon I won't be there. I have some things to take care of. I'll get something to eat while I'm out."

"That sounds mysterious," Jason said, rising from his desk and pulling his jacket from the back of his chair. "Care to explain?"

Jeff picked up the bank deposit bag, and they both headed to their cars. "I'll talk to you and Sharon when I get home."

"Now I'm really curious," Jason said, opening his car door.

"Don't worry," Jeff said. "I'll see you soon." He watched in his rearview mirror as his son pulled out of the parking space behind the store. He sat for a moment while his car idled. He was certain about his next step. He just had to drop off the deposit and then call his realtor.

Jeff put his car in gear and set out.

"HEY, DAD," Sharon said as she started the dishwasher. "We were getting worried about you. It's not like you to stay out so late."

Jeff walked over to his daughter-in-law and gave her a quick peck on the cheek. "It's only nine o'clock. I think a sixty-three-year-old man is safe being on the streets at such an hour."

Sharon gave him a rueful smile. "Of course you are," she said. "It's just not like you, that's all."

"Kids in bed?"

"Just," Sharon said as she began to wipe the countertops.

"Where's Jason?"

"He's right here," Jason said from the kitchen doorway. "You can go up to say goodnight to the kids. They won't be asleep yet."

Jeff shook his head. "I'd like to talk to the two of you. Can we sit at the table?" He pulled out a chair and sat at the kitchen table. Sharon looked at her husband with wide eyes, and he shrugged. They took seats opposite Jeff.

"What's up?" Jason asked.

"First off, I want to thank both of you for welcoming me into your home after my house sold so quickly."

Sharon smiled at him. "We've loved having you here. You've been a tremendous help with Tyler and Talia. We're all going to miss you terribly when you move into that new house of yours —even though it's only a mile and a half away."

"That's what I wanted to talk to you about." Jeff took a deep breath before he continued. "I'm not moving into that house. I canceled my escrow." He looked at Jason. "That's what I was doing tonight."

"Why?" he asked. "I thought it was perfect for you."

"It would've been perfect for Millie and me—but not for me, on my own."

"Okay." Sharon sat back and began to twirl a strand of chestnut hair that had escaped her topknot. "That's no problem. You can stay with us until you find exactly what you want."

"That's just it—I don't know what I want. And I don't think I'm going to figure it out while I'm living in your guest room and working at the hardware store." He looked into the earnest eyes of the two people whom he loved so much. "I need a change of scenery—I need distance from my old life to figure out what my next chapter will be." He looked at his hands. "Your mother and I had a wonderful marriage, and I loved being her husband. I think I'm finally ready to be part of a couple again. I don't think I can do that until I know what I want from the rest of my life."

They sat in silence as his words sunk in.

"I've loved being here—don't get me wrong." He looked at Sharon. "You've never made me feel like an imposition or like I'm in your way."

"That's because you haven't been!" Her voice wavered. "I love you!"

"What does this mean, Dad? What are you going to do?"

"I've decided to take an extended road trip. You both know how much I love to drive. I've always found it easy to think when I'm on the open road. I'll go wherever my fancy takes me. I know I'd like to drive up the California coast. Maybe I'll even want to settle down in one of those laid-back beach towns."

"You wouldn't," Sharon cried. "That'd be way too far from home. The kids would be devastated."

"Or you might all love spending a month with me in the summer." He shook his head. "I'm not sure I'm a beach kind of guy. The point is—I need to discover what I want."

"Fair enough," Jason said, struggling to keep his voice even. "When do you plan to go?"

"I'll stay until the kids are on Christmas break. I want to go to Tyler's band concert, and I want to see Talia in the school play."

"Oh, good," Sharon said. "And you'll still go with us to my parents' for Christmas?"

"No. I've decided to set out on the day after break starts."

"But Mom ..."

Jeff held up his hand. "Your folks are wonderful people, and

33

I'm very fond of them. I appreciate their invitation, but I've decided to spend the holidays with my cousin Dave and his wife in Phoenix. They've been after me for years to spend time with them there during the winter."

"So, you won't be alone for Christmas?" she asked.

"Definitely not. Please give my regards to your parents. The six of you will have a wonderful time, and I'll expect a nice, long call on Christmas Day. We can do one of those video things."

"And after the holidays?" Jason asked.

Jeff reached across the table and placed a hand on top of each of theirs. "I'll head out and see where life takes me. I've been thinking about this for a long time. I feel like there's something out there for me—something that will fill the rest of my days with joy—but I have to leave home to find it."

CHAPTER 6

"I got here about fifteen minutes ago," Judy said as she opened the door to let Maggie in. Her head snapped up. "Hi, John. I didn't expect to see you here. Don't you spend Sunday afternoons watching a football game on TV?"

"I figured you two might need help wrangling some of that junk in the attic. I figured I'd lend a hand and leave you to it. I'll be home in time for the second half."

"I've said it before, and I'll say it again—you've married the perfect man, Maggie." She turned, and they followed her up the stairs. "I really appreciate this, John."

"You're right—he's a gem." Maggie bumped shoulders with him playfully. "I brought some battery-operated lanterns from Rosemont. We keep them for when the power goes out."

"There's plenty of light in the turret room," Judy said, "but the attic is pitch black. With John's help, we can haul anything we want to look at out of the attic and examine it there."

THEY STEPPED into the turret room. Sunshine streamed in from the windows on three sides, making the black hole that was the attic seem even darker. They switched on their lanterns and flashlights and began to sift through the jumble of items in front of them.

"It's almost three," Maggie called to John as he manhandled a trunk at the far end of the attic. "I don't want you to miss the second half."

"It's all right," he called back, his voice evidencing exertion. "I want to finish clearing a path to this window." He pointed behind him to a window at the opposite end of the attic. "The shutters are closed on the outside, but when they're open, you'll have a good amount of light in here."

He stood and wiped his hand across his brow. "I know the two of you too well. This is not the only time you're going to be in this attic today."

"You've got our number." Judy chuckled. "I'll ask Sam to open the shutters."

"I'll move this dresser to one side, and then I'm done," John said.

Maggie held a lantern over her head while she and Judy examined John's handiwork. Boxes labeled in neat block letters as FILES, RECORDS, LETTERS, or RECEIPTS were lined up on one side of the newly cleared path through the center of the attic. Next to them were trunks. On the other side of the attic were pieces of discarded furniture and bins labeled KITCHEN, CHINA, HOUSEHOLD, and CHRISTMAS.

John made his way to the door to the attic, wiping his hands on his jeans. Maggie and Judy followed him into the turret room.

He squinted in the brilliant sunshine pouring through the windows and pointed to the boxes and bins that they'd had him move out of the attic. "Are you sure this is all you want out of there? I'm about to take off."

"That's everything," Judy assured him. "You're going to be late as it is. Thank you so much for helping me with this."

"If I've learned one thing about the two of you, it's that you're irresistibly drawn to an attic. No point in fighting it."

Maggie cuffed him playfully on the arm and moved to the head of the stairs.

"I can see myself out," John said. "Call me if you need anything." He leaned in and kissed his wife on the cheek. "If you're not home by six, I'm coming back to get you."

"We'll be done long before then. We shouldn't need more than an hour or two," Judy assured him. "Don't worry about a thing."

Judy and Maggie set to work on the boxes stacked in the turret room before John had made it out the front door. They unpacked two cartons of fine china, complete with creme pots, soup tureens, and twenty-four scallop-edged Copeland Spode dessert plates. A third box contained a set of Royal Winton chintz ware.

Judy inhaled sharply when she unwrapped the first piece. "Look at this," she said, holding a teacup up by its delicate handle. "I'll need to do some research, but I think this is part of an early twentieth-century English breakfast set."

"Incredible," Maggie said, reaching for the cup and turning it over in her hand. "Are you sure you want to unpack all of that?" She gestured to the array of china they'd already unwrapped and stacked along the walls under the window.

"I'm too curious—I can't stop myself. I think we'll have just enough room to set out what's in this box." Judy reached for the next piece. "I know it seems silly. I'll probably end up rewrapping all of this and putting it back in the attic, but I want to see it."

"Me, too," Maggie said. "Let's take photos of everything. If it's valuable—as I'm sure most of this is—you'll want to insure it."

"Good point!" Judy exclaimed. "Who's that appraiser guy you used to help you sell the silver you found in Rosemont's attic? Maybe I should call him."

"Gordon Mortimer. I'll get you his number. He'll know about all of this, and if you want to sell any of it, he can help you."

"Thank you." Judy handed Maggie the last piece of china from the box.

They both sat back on their haunches and admired the display.

"It's all lovely," Maggie said, "but my favorite is that chintz ware. I love the pinks and yellows."

"So cheerful, isn't it?" Judy said. "I'm going to keep it and use it. I think I'll have you and Joan, Susan—and Nancy Knudsen, too—over for tea when I get this place fixed up. And I'll use this china."

"That's a perfect plan. I'll look forward to it." She checked her watch. "It's after four thirty. The light's beginning to fade. We should knock off. I don't want John sending the posse after us."

"That's for sure. There's only one more box that I'd like to peek in before we go," Judy said. She stood and retrieved a cardboard box labeled "FOR JEFFREY."

"Let's just take a quick look." Judy unfolded the well-worn flaps. "It looks like someone opened and closed this box many times."

The two women peered inside. "There's a bunch of round objects, wrapped in tissue," Judy said.

"They're tied with red ribbons, and each one has a tag attached. They must have been gifts." Maggie speculated.

Judy removed one tissue-wrapped package. "It's light-weight," she said as she turned the tag to the light and read the words. "To Jeffrey. I hope this one day finds its way to you. With great love and blessings." The tag was signed, "Uncle William." She held the tag out to Maggie.

"It looks like the same handwriting on each of these boxes. Very neat and precise. Almost like the person was a draftsman." She raised her eyes to Judy. "You look like you've seen a ghost. Do you want to see what's in there?"

"I think I already know." Judy untied the red ribbon and care-fully peeled back the tissue. There, in the center, sat an intricately carved wooden snowflake ornament. She turned it over in her hand and ran a finger over the velvety smooth, sanded surface.

Maggie gasped. "That's gorgeous. I've never seen anything like it."

"I have," Judy said, turning a tearful gaze to her friend. "I inherited a box of ornaments like these from my mother."

Maggie looked at her quizzically.

Judy launched into the tale of the gifts in the alcove. "And every Monday before Christmas, William would leave one of these." Judy pointed to the box. "Each one was completely unique. No two were the same."

"That's incredible."

Judy set the ornament aside and began removing the other tissue-wrapped packages from the box. "Some of my happiest Christmas memories were unwrapping William's snowflakes with my mother. When I was twelve, she actually closed the shop early—I don't think she or my grandmother had ever done that before—and we made hot chocolates. By then there were enough snowflakes to decorate a small tree, and after we unwrapped the newest snowflake, she handed me the box we kept them all in and pointed to a tree in the window. It was the first time she ever let me help with the window display."

Judy handed Maggie one of the last packages in the box. "Of course, I don't hang them up anymore."

"Why not?"

"I got tired of telling people the darned things weren't for sale."

Maggie laughed.

"I'm sorry this Jeffrey never got to see his ornament," Judy picked up the unwrapped ornament again. "Who are the other ornaments for?"

"All the tags say the same thing."

"He must have carved an ornament for us and this Jeffrey—his nephew—every year."

"I'll bet you're right," Maggie said. "How sad that he never got to give them to this boy who he evidently loved a great deal."

Judy turned her head aside and sniffed.

Maggie rubbed her friend's back. "It's very tender, isn't it? And you know what? I think you were meant to find this box of ornaments. You can add them to your collection. I'm sure that would make William happy."

Judy shook her head. "I'm not going to keep these." She swallowed hard and looked at her friend. "I'm going to find this Jeffrey and give him these ornaments. That sweet man wanted his nephew to have them, and I'm going to do my darnedest to make it happen."

A smile spread across Maggie's face. "I love that. There's something so poetically right about it."

"I don't know how I'm going to do it." Judy sighed heavily.

"You won't have to figure this out alone," Maggie said. "Why don't you email Susan tonight? She'll have suggestions on how to find him."

Judy pulled out her cell phone and took photos of the box of treasures they'd uncovered. She rewrapped the ornament and put it into her purse. "We're going to find your Jeffrey for you, Mr. Olsson," she said, looking to the top of the turret. "We're going to make your Christmas wish come true."

CHAPTER 7

*J*udy stopped abruptly on the sidewalk and rummaged in her purse for her phone. The incoming call announcement feature told her that Susan Scanlon was calling, and she was anxious to hear from her attorney. "Hi, Susan," she said breathlessly into the phone.

"Did I get you at a bad time?"

"No. I'm just walking home to pick up the salad I made to take to book club tonight. Are you going?"

"I am. Gosh, I didn't realize it was getting so late. I'm bringing an apple streusel pie from Laura's Bakery. I've got to get out of here to pick it up. I was calling to update you on what I've found out about Jeffrey."

Judy drew in a deep breath. "And?"

"I'm sorry, but I didn't uncover anything. The real property records listed William Olsson as the owner until the treasurer's deed put the title into your name. He died without a will, as you know, and all of the probate records were destroyed years ago."

"That's why the treasurer never found the person who inherited it from William."

"Exactly," Susan said. "I didn't think there would be much chance we'd find anything useful."

"I really want to send these ornaments to Jeffrey. Any idea what I might do now?"

"Why don't you post a photo of one of the ornaments on social media? Maybe someone will know him. Ask people to share your post."

"Good idea. I've heard of people finding the rightful owners of all sorts of things that way," Judy said. "Wedding rings, military medals, pets."

"I know how important this is to you. It's worth a try," Susan said. "I'm going to let you go. I don't want to be late for our discussion. *Guiding Emily* was the best book I've read in a long time. Loved the Garth character! Who wouldn't like a seeing eye dog who thinks like a person?"

"Me, too," Judy replied. "See you soon. And thank you for trying to find Jeffrey." She quickened her pace and turned onto her street. She usually walked past her home and down the block to the Olsson house. She liked to open it up and stare into the interior, imagining the possibilities of the space. She'd have to forego this pleasure tonight. It was past time to grab her salad out of the fridge and head to Lyla Kershaw's for the meeting that was the highlight of her month.

Later that evening, after the congenial group of friends had consumed the potluck supper and finished their discussion of this month's book, they settled into Lyla's living room with their pie and coffee. Lyla's new husband, Robert Harris, had just lit the fire for them.

"There's a ton of food in the kitchen," Lyla said, kissing him on the cheek. "Help yourself and come join us."

"I'll fix myself a plate, but I don't want to butt in on all this girl talk."

"We'd love to have you join us," Sunday Sloan said, going up to Robert and hugging him. As the rare-book librarian at Highpointe College, she and Robert had become friends when he had held a similar post at the University of Cambridge in England. Robert was now a rare book seller, operating an internet business located in Westbury. Sunday still marveled at the strange turn of events that had brought the older man to Westbury and reunited him with his long-lost love, Lyla Kershaw. The fact that Robert and Lyla were the biological parents of Sunday's boyfriend, Josh Newlon, made the couple more like family than friends or coworkers.

"Actually, I'd like you to hear the story I'm about to tell the group," Judy said, placing her coffee cup on an end table as she settled into a chair flanking the fire. She looked around the room as Susan and Maggie claimed the sofa and Joan took the chair on the other side of the fireplace. Lyla sat in the remaining chair, and Robert perched on the arm.

"Do you mind if I go first?" Judy said. "We always catch up with each other's lives when we come in here for dessert, and I have something big I want to tell all of you."

The room grew quiet.

"Most of you know that I recently bought the Olsson house."

Lyla's head jerked back. "*The* Olsson house?"

Judy nodded. "I bought it at a tax sale last spring, and the title got transferred into my name a couple of weeks ago."

"How exciting!" Sunday said.

"Sam's still inspecting it for me," Judy said. "I'm terrified that I've bought a bottomless money pit. Time will tell. In the meantime, Maggie and I were exploring in the attic and found all sorts of cool stuff—including this."

Judy reached into her purse and removed a round package wrapped in tissue. She pulled the tissue aside and held out the ornament.

"That's exquisite," Robert said. "May I?"

Judy handed it to him.

"We found an entire box of these Christmas decorations." She told them about the notes to a nephew named Jeffrey and the set of ornaments that William had given to her family.

Robert handed the wooden snowflake to Lyla. She turned it over in her hands, inspecting it from every angle, before passing the treasure to Sunday.

"You can understand why I'm so anxious to get these to the Jeffrey they were carved for, whoever he is."

"Of course," Lyla said.

"Susan's searched all public records, and we're at a dead end. The only thing left for me to do is to post it on social media to see if I can find the rightful owner." She looked at the faces of her friends staring intently at her. "I'm asking you to share my post with your friends. I understand that's how things 'go viral.' Will you do that for me?"

Heads nodded in agreement.

Sunday and Robert exchanged a look.

"I think we can do better than that," Sunday said. "Robert and I'll do some digging for this Jeffrey. The library is full of all sorts of information."

"Really?" Judy asked. "But I don't even have his last name. What can you do with just his first name?"

"We librarians—and former librarians—don't want to give away our secrets," Robert said, smiling at Judy. "Sunday and I will put our heads together. Do your social media posts, and Sunday and I will get busy."

"You think you'll find him?" Judy sat forward in her chair and clasped her hands together.

"It's a long shot," Sunday said, "but this past year has taught me to believe in luck." She went to Judy and knelt next to her, looking into her eyes. "We'll get started tomorrow. Keep the faith."

CHAPTER 8

*J*udy was placing On Sale stickers on turkeys, pumpkins, and other fall-themed decorations when the phone rang. She abandoned her task and answered with a cheerful "Celebrations—how can we help?"

"Judy? It's Sunday."

"Hello, dear." Judy braced herself for unwelcome news. It'd been two weeks since the book club meeting. Sunday must be calling to tell her they hadn't been able to dig up any information. "How are y—"

"I think we've found him!"

Judy almost dropped the phone.

"We've got two men we think you should contact. One of them may very well be your Jeffrey."

"Gosh—really?" Judy sank against the counter by the cash register and blew out a breath. "That's wonderful news. I was sure you were calling to tell me you'd come up empty-handed."

"Nope. It took a bit of doing, but we've got two names and email addresses for you. Robert is sure that one of them is our guy, and I think the other is." Sunday chuckled. "He and I have even placed a bet—if one of them is the right man, the other has to buy dinner."

"I'm buying you both dinner—whether either one turns out to be my Jeffrey or not. How did you find these names?"

"Robert searched through records of the *Westbury Gazette* after WWII. He found a society page article about the wedding of an Alma Olsson to Erik Carson. The reception was held at the Olsson home. I've scanned the article and am going to send it to you. It's got some lovely photos of the house and garden from that period."

"I would love to see that!"

"Anyway, the article reported that the newlyweds were going to settle in Cleveland. I checked for Jeffrey Carsons in Cleveland and came up with quite a few candidates. We narrowed the list down by age and there are two men who are the right age to be your Jeffrey. One of them used to own a hardware store, and the other is still a college professor."

"I don't know what to say. I guess I didn't believe you'd find anything."

Sunday clicked her tongue. "Don't doubt your librarian!"

Judy laughed. "I guess not. I'm so very grateful. And I mean it—I'm taking you and Josh and Robert and Lyla to dinner. You've made my day!"

"I'll send you the contact information of these two Jeffrey Carsons, together with what we found out about them."

"What should I do now? Email them?"

"Exactly. I saw your social media post about the ornament. I'd use what you wrote there and attach a photo of the ornament. Good luck—and let me know what happens. I think one of these is your man."

Later that night, after writing and revising her email at least a dozen times, Judy pushed send and off her emails went to the Jeffrey Carsons in Cleveland. She took off her reading glasses and rubbed her tired eyes. There was nothing more for her to do.

Judy brushed her teeth and got into her pajamas before double-checking the locks on her doors. Her computer screen sat dark on her desk in the corner of her kitchen. She glanced at the wall clock. It was almost midnight. She wouldn't have gotten any responses yet.

She bent over her keyboard and logged in. Her screen came to life, and she opened her email account. One new message awaited. Her hand shook as she fumbled with the mouse to click on the response from the college professor.

He stated simply that his family had no affiliation with any Olssons or Westbury. He wished her well on her quest to find the owner of the ornament.

Judy clicked back to the inbox; all her hopes were now pinned to the other Jeffrey Carson. With any luck, she'd hear from him soon.

CHAPTER 9

Sam lunged for the paper plate as it began pinwheeling down the table, driven by a brisk breeze that had suddenly sprung up. People at the tables around them were doing the same thing. "Looks like the first snowstorm of the season is on its way into town." He gestured to the sky with his head.

"They're predicting three inches by morning," Joan said. "It's uncanny how the weather is always clear and sunny for the Fairview Terraces Thanksgiving Prayer Breakfast, but as soon as the service is done and we all finish breakfast, the temperature drops, and the wind picks up."

Sam took Judy's plate and placed it, and Joan's, on top of his own. "I'll take these to the trash."

"Thank you," Judy said. "I think that wind is sending everyone packing." The three hundred people gathered on the sweeping front lawn of the retirement community were hastily dispersing. Judy gathered up their paper coffee cups as she and Joan stood. "This was lovely. I always like starting Thanksgiving this way. It reminds me of the larger meaning of the day."

"I agree," Joan said, and they began to crunch across the dormant lawn to the parking lot. "I prepped the bird before we came. All I have to do now is stick it in the oven and peel potatoes. I made cranberry relish and a pumpkin pie yesterday."

"I've got a salad, dinner rolls, and my mother's sweet potatoes all set to go," Judy said. "I was thinking of trying a new recipe, but ..." She was interrupted by someone calling her name.

Judy turned to find Sunday Sloan, walking hand-in-hand with Josh Newlon, approaching her.

Joan smiled at the couple and leaned into Judy. "I've got to get the bird started," she said. "I'm going to scoot. See you around three? I thought we'd eat at four. Is that too early?"

"Suits me just fine," Judy said. "I don't run Black Friday promotions, but Celebrations will be crazy busy tomorrow. I plan to be at the shop early, so I'm delighted to have somewhere low-key to go today."

"See you soon," Joan said, moving away from Judy.

"Happy Thanksgiving," Judy said as Sunday and Josh joined her. "I'm so glad you came this morning."

"It was my first time," Sunday said. "I think I'm going to make it an annual tradition." She looked at Josh, and he nodded his agreement. "I don't want to hold you up, but I was wondering if you'd had any replies to your emails?"

Judy's smile dimmed. "I got one right away from the college professor—he's not the man I'm looking for. I never heard back from the other guy. It's been almost two weeks, so I assume I'm not going to."

Sunday reached over and touched Judy's elbow. "Darn it! Why don't you send the email again? What can it hurt? If you still have no response by Monday, I'll go back to the drawing board."

"I hate to ask you to do that," Judy replied. "I may just have to face the fact that I'm not going to find him."

"I'm sorry. I was so hopeful."

"It's not your fault," Judy said. "I'll resend the email. As you said, what can it hurt?"

"That's the spirit! I can't shake the feeling that you're going to find the right Jeffrey."

CHAPTER 10

*J*eff took his seat along one side of the table, next to his son at the end. Sharon was at the other end, and a large, golden turkey took center stage on a platter in front of Jason. Jeff swallowed hard. He remembered when he and Millie had occupied the positions that were now filled by the younger couple—and the pride at having produced such a beautiful meal and the exhaustion from the effort, as well.

Thanksgiving was yet another poignant reminder of the changing of the guard. This sense of displacement would have happened even if Millie had been alive, he reminded himself. It just would have been easier to accept this passage into a new phase of life if she'd been at his side. They'd have joked and laughed, and somehow, he wouldn't have been left feeling that life was slipping through his fingers.

Talia's voice jolted him back to the present. He smiled into the eyes of his granddaughter. "What was that, honey? Sometimes Grandpa doesn't hear so well." He pointed to his ears in an attempt to cover up his inattention.

"Would you like white or dark meat or both?" she asked. She looked toward her father, who was bent over the bird, a large fork in one hand and a carving knife in the other.

"Some of each, please," he said. "This all looks fabulous, Sharon. You've outdone yourself."

She grinned. "You say that every year."

"That's because you always do," Jeff said, accepting a plate from his son piled high with fragrant turkey. He helped himself to mashed potatoes and passed the bowl to Sharon.

"I was wondering," he said to his grandkids, "if you could help me with my new tablet? I bought it to keep in touch with you while I'm on my trip, but I haven't figured out how to set it up. I can't even get my email, and I have no idea about Facebook."

"Sure," Tyler said. "It'll be a piece of cake."

"Why aren't you coming with us?" Talia asked. "I've never had a Christmas without you, Grandpa." Her voice wavered. "Don't you want to be with us anymore?"

"We've discussed this," Jason said. "Your grandfather still loves us all very much. He has to do this for himself, and when you love someone, you encourage them to do what they need for themselves."

"I know," Talia said, picking at her plate. "I'm sorry, Grandpa. I want you to have a good time."

"We can do FaceTime—or whatever it's called—on my tablet, and we can talk and see each other every day. It'll be like we're together. And I'll be home before you know it."

Talia nodded sullenly.

"Tell me again what the two of you want for Christmas," Jeff said. "I think I forgot."

Talia straightened in her chair. "I really want those ice skates ..."

~

"ANOTHER PIECE OF PIE, DAD?" Jason pulled the foil back from the pie plate on the counter. "There're only two pieces left."

Jeff patted his stomach. "I shouldn't, but ..."

"It's Thanksgiving. Calories don't count; you know that." Sharon put her hands on her lower back and stretched. "The kids are asleep, and I'm pooped." She walked over and brushed a kiss on the top of Jeff's head. "I'm turning in."

"I'm going to finish up this piece of pie, and then I'll be right behind you," Jason said. "We'll be busy tomorrow with sales of Christmas lights and tree stands."

The two men attacked their pieces of pie with purpose.

"I'll put these plates in the dishwasher," Jeff said, pulling his new tablet across the table to him. "Now that I know how, I think I'll check my email before I hit the hay. I haven't looked at it in more than a month."

"It'll take hours for you to catch up," Jason said.

"Actually, son, I'll be amazed if I have more than a dozen emails—and all of them will be trying to sell me something."

Jason yawned. "I'll leave you to it. See you tomorrow. And don't feel like you have to be at the store first thing. Sleep in and get there whenever."

"I'm bushed, myself, so I'll take you up on that offer. I hope you don't say that to all of your employees." Jeff grinned.

"Only the one who taught me everything I know." Jason patted his father on the back. "'Night, Dad."

Jeff opened the case on the tablet, hoping he'd remember how to log on the way his grandchildren had just taught him.

His screen came to life, and he clicked on his email icon. As expected, most of the messages were easily dismissed. However, one of them—sent two weeks earlier and then, again, that afternoon—caught his eye.

Jeff opened the message and read it and then reread it. Could this possibly be true? He clicked on the attached photo of the ornament, and his breath caught in his throat.

He stood quickly, almost knocking the kitchen chair over, and took the tablet into his room. He set the ornament he'd removed from the garage sale on the bed, next to his tablet, confirming what he already knew.

Suddenly, Jeff didn't feel tired anymore. He typed his reply to this incredibly kind woman named Judy. She'd gone to great lengths to find him and restore this part of his past to him. He didn't know why he was so excited about this—surely his focus should be on his future, not on his childhood.

He clicked the Send button, and happiness surged through him. Here was one more thing to be thankful for.

Judy padded to her kitchen door in her slippers. Her satchel stood on the mat, and she'd dug her snow boots out of the back of the closet. She was ready to head out before seven the next morning.

She forced herself to walk past her computer—she'd checked her email when she'd gotten home from Joan and Sam's earlier in the evening. There'd been no response to her email, and it was ridiculous to think that anyone would respond on Thanksgiving night.

Unable to help herself, she circled back and logged on. Her eyes widened when she saw the response and then filled with tears as she read it. She'd found him! Jeffrey was out there! He had a matching ornament and would send her a photo of it when his grandkids woke up and helped him figure out how. She smiled at this. He sounded as proficient with the computer as she was. He'd given her his phone number, too, and invited her to call him—the next night, if it would be convenient for her.

Her fingers fumbled on the keys, and she deleted and retyped her short reply several times: She'd love to talk to him and would call him at seven.

Judy logged off and headed to her bedroom with a light heart. She now had something to look forward to tomorrow other than just a busy day in retail during the holidays.

CHAPTER 11

*J*udy muted the Christmas movie playing on her television and tucked her feet up under herself on the sofa. This call wouldn't take more than a few minutes, and then she'd be back to escaping into the happily-ever-after world of her movie. She placed the call.

Jeff was pacing in his son's living room, waiting for the phone to ring. He was grateful that Jason and his family had all gone out for pizza and a movie, affording him privacy for his call. For reasons he couldn't put his finger on, he hadn't told them about finding the ornament or the intriguing email from the woman claiming to have an entire box of them—all made for Jeff decades ago. He answered on the first ring.

"Hello, Judy." He bit his lip. What should he say now?

"Hi, Jeff."

He thought there was hesitancy in her voice. Maybe she was as nervous as he was.

"How was your Thanksgiving?" They said it at the same time and laughed. That seemed to break the tension.

"Ladies first?" Jeff said.

Judy swallowed the expected reply. "I spent it with my best friend and her husband—that was very nice—but I have to be honest; I find most holidays to be very lonely affairs." She instantly wished she hadn't confessed to this. Now he'd think she was a sad, old crone.

Jeff chuckled. "Honestly—that's exactly how I feel. Ever since my wife died a little more than three years ago, I've felt adrift—especially at this time of year. I was with my son and his family—he's married to a wonderful woman and I have two grandchildren—so it was all very nice. But it's just not the same."

"I'm so sorry about your wife. I lost my husband almost thirty years ago in a car accident. I've lived most of my adult life as a single woman, but I still miss him. The thing that helps me get through the holidays is that I own a retail store—I'm so busy at the shop that I can't think straight."

"I own—used to own—a hardware store. I took it over from my dad and recently sold my interest to my son. Hardware stores don't really have a Christmas rush."

"You haven't missed much," Judy said, pulling an afghan from the back of the sofa over her feet and making herself comfortable. "That's three things we have in common. The ornament, having lost a spouse, and owning a family retail business. My mom left me the shop when she died."

Jeff settled into his favorite recliner and pushed back on the arms to activate the footrest. "Tell me about your store."

"Celebrations is a small gift shop, located on our historic town square in Westbury. I sell stationery, invitations, and gifts. I started working there when I was a child—dusting shelves and straightening the inventory. By the time I went away to college, I was running the register and closing in the evening."

"Were you a business major? Did you plan to come back after college?"

Judy laughed. "Nope—the business aspects of owning the shop have all been learned by experience. The school of hard knocks and all that. I was an art major and had big dreams of becoming a famous sculptor. I married in college, and we planned to move to Paris after graduation—to live in an artist's grotto—the whole bit."

"I gather you didn't do that. What happened?"

"My mother became extremely ill with cancer. My father died when I was seven, so there was no one else to care for her and keep the shop open. I took an incomplete in my classes and moved back home. It was supposed to be temporary. My husband stayed to finish the semester." Her voice grew hoarse. "He was killed the week after I got home. My mom recovered and returned to the shop, but I sunk into a deep depression. I stayed on while I grieved. By the time I was ready to return to school, Mom relapsed and then passed away. She left me the shop and my childhood home—that's where I'm talking to you from. I found I have a knack for merchandising—I guess that's where I use my artistic talent. I know this isn't the dream I left home to pursue, but I love my life."

"Whew," Jeff said. "I have a similar backstory. I wanted to be an architect from the time I was little. That's what I was studying in college. I made it to my last year when my father died of a heart attack. I'm an only child, so I came right home. Like you, I had worked at the store from the time I could walk. I thought I would help my mother learn the business and then go back to my studies. My next semester was supposed to be spent abroad, and I was so excited about it. I'd always wanted to see the incredible architecture of Europe." He paused.

"So, you didn't go back, either. What happened?"

"My mother wasn't able to cope with handling the business. Dad had a very capable store manager, but she ran him off. Mom was prone to mercurial mood swings and was impossible to be around. That's one of the reasons I'd been so keen to go to Europe. Looking back, I'd say she was bipolar. We didn't know much about mental health issues, back in the day."

"You're right about that. Depression, anxiety, addiction—our society has done a poor job of helping people suffering from these things. But it's getting better."

They were silent for a moment, then Judy continued. "So, did you give up your dream and run the store?"

"I did. I married my wife, and we had the son I've told you about, and it's been a grand life. I wouldn't trade any of it."

"What happened to your mother?"

"She became a recluse and a hoarder. The only person she even barely tolerated was my wife. She wouldn't see me or even talk to me on the phone. When Millie began treatment for cancer, she wasn't well enough to see my mom. I was over-whelmed with Millie's care, and when my mom died—the year before Millie passed—I hadn't seen her in years."

"That must have been hard on you."

"I blame myself for not doing more for my mother."

"You can't force someone to accept help. Sometimes people are on journeys that we wouldn't choose for them, but we have to let them live their lives," Judy said. "You said in your email that you found the ornament in your mother's things?"

"Yes. I sold Mom's house, furniture and all, and had her personal effects boxed up and sent to me. I put them in storage and didn't touch them. I'd forgotten about the ornament—I hadn't seen it in decades—until last fall when my son and daughter-in-law helped me with a garage sale. In fact, I found it in a bin, priced to sell."

"Oh, no!" Judy looked at the box containing the wooden ornaments that William had carved for his nephew. "Do you remember your uncle?"

"Very vaguely. He stopped at our home one Christmas when he first came to this country from Sweden. He brought me the ornament that I sent you the photo of. He said that he made it. I remember being fascinated with it as a child."

"So, William and Alma were on good terms?"

"At the time," Jeff said, "but like she did with everyone else, she became suspicious of him and paranoid, and finally cut him out of her life."

"The notes on these ornaments testify to the fact that your uncle loved you a great deal. He never forgot you, Jeff."

Jeff swallowed hard against the lump in his throat.

"You *must* have these in time for Christmas," Judy said, sensing his emotion. "Where can I send them to you? I'm happy to use an overnight delivery service, and I'll insure them. Just give me an address. I'll get them out tomorrow."

Jeff had answered the call planning to ask Judy to mail the ornaments to Jason's house at his expense. So, he was surprised to hear himself say, "Do you mind if I pick them up? I'm starting a road trip in about three weeks. I'm going to end up with my cousin in Phoenix for Christmas, and I'll be driving right by Westbury on the way." He winced as he said this since he knew Westbury was at least two hundred miles out of his way. He hoped she wouldn't realize that.

"Sure," she said. "I'm not going anywhere during the holiday rush. I've always wanted to close the shop for a week during January and go somewhere warm, like Phoenix. One of these years, I'm going to do it!"

"Great. I don't want to risk the ornaments getting lost in the mail," Jeff said. "And I'd love to meet you. I've enjoyed talking to you."

"Me, too. This has been fun. I'll keep them in the back room at Celebrations. I'll email you the address."

"Terrific." He did some quick mileage calculations in his head. "I'll plan to be there in the middle of the day on the twenty-first." That would allow him ample time to complete his drive to Phoenix.

"I'll be at the shop."

"I'm looking forward to meeting you," Jeff reiterated.

"Have a safe trip. See you soon." Judy swiped to end the call and clutched the phone to her chest. He was just stopping by on his way to Phoenix, she reminded herself. And he didn't live anywhere near Westbury. She glanced at the television, where a new movie with the same plot and happy ending was playing out on the screen. What she longed for only happened in the movies, not in real life. She snatched the remote from the end table, clicked off the television, and headed to bed.

CHAPTER 12

*J*udy placed the box of ornaments under the worktable in the back room at Celebrations. It would be safe there until Jeff arrived to pick them up. He'd texted her early that morning to tell her that he was on his way and anticipated stopping by around three the next afternoon.

Celebrations had seen a steady stream of customers all day, but now, in the late afternoon, the shop was quiet. Judy straightened the shelves and restocked her display of Christmas tea towels. She found herself wondering if Jeff would be impressed, then quickly shook the idea out of her head. What difference would it make what he thought?

She stepped onto the sidewalk, window cleaner in hand, and sprayed and wiped the plate glass on the door until it sparkled. She moved on to the large display window. The afternoon was sunny, but the air had a nip to it. Wishing she'd slipped into her jacket, she gazed into her Christmas display and admired her handiwork. The tall, slim tree sparkled with its white beaded garland and silver ornaments that added shine without being gaudy. Artificial snow at the tree's base was studded with ceramic woodland creatures decorated with colorful bows, ivy, and berries. She usually included Santa and his reindeer in her window but hadn't been moved to do so this year. She slung her rag over her shoulder and pondered the window. It still needed something.

Her head suddenly snapped back. "Of course!" she said out loud. Judy knew how she'd spend her evening. She checked her watch—she had forty-five minutes until closing.

Judy spent that forty-five minutes dragging a small artificial tree out of her storage closet and assembling it. She couldn't remember the last time she'd used the tree. She fluffed the branches and held her breath when she plugged the lights into a socket. They still worked!

Judy scooted the tall tree in the display window to one side and rearranged the ceramic animals. The newly assembled tree fit into the space perfectly. She checked her watch and noted that it was two minutes past closing. She flipped the sign on the door from Open to Closed and set out.

THIRTY MINUTES LATER, Judy pulled to the curb in front of her shop. She'd changed into jeans and a sweatshirt, eaten a carton of yogurt and an apple, and returned to Celebrations with *her* box of the carved wooden ornaments. Jeff might take the time to unwrap and look at all of his ornaments, but he wouldn't have a tree to put them on. This way, he could see what his treasures looked like in the way William had intended them to be seen.

Judy unwrapped her ornaments carefully, admiring each

one. She hadn't displayed them at the shop for many years. People were always trying to buy them—and she was unwilling to part with even one of them. She used to put them on a tree at home but hadn't bothered with her own Christmas tree for several years.

She placed the ornaments on the tree in the window, taking great care to position each one so that it hung freely and wasn't obscured by any of the branches. She stepped outside to view the window and decided to adjust the track lighting that ran along the window's top front edge. The tree needed to be the focal point of the window.

Judy went back inside and set up her step ladder. She had to stand on the top wrung to adjust the lights, but she wanted the tree to be perfectly illuminated.

She was on her fifth trip up the ladder when her cell phone rang in her purse. She stepped down the rungs as fast as she dared, telling herself not to get excited. It was probably a robo-call. She lunged for her phone.

"Hel … hello," she said, breathing hard and choking on the word.

"Hi, Judy. It's Jeff. Have I caught you at a bad time?"

Judy brushed a lock of hair out of her eyes and tucked it behind her ear. "No. This is fine." She took a deep breath. "I was just … rearranging inventory."

"I remember those days," he said. "The work never ends when you own a store. I'm sorry to interrupt you. I just wanted to let you know that I made good time today, and I've stopped for the night. I plan to get an early start tomorrow and should see you in the early afternoon."

"I'm so happy to hear that. I hope you get a good night's sleep. I never do well in a strange bed."

"I don't either. I've brought my pillow from home," he said.

"That always helps." He paused before continuing. "I'm really looking forward to meeting you."

Judy felt the tension drain out from between her shoulder blades. There was something about his voice that made her feel calm. "I can't wait, either. Everything's all ready for you," she said, smiling at the surprise she'd set up for him in her window. "Thanks for letting me know how you're doing."

"I'll see you soon," he said.

"Goodnight. Safe travels tomorrow."

CHAPTER 13

*J*udy was winding the cord around the vacuum cleaner when she heard her phone ping. She pulled it out of the pocket of her jeans and tapped the screen. Jeff was on his way. It was just seven o'clock.

She'd have barely enough time to clean the small bathroom and take the trash out before she had to go back home to shower and get dressed for work. She knew Jeff would only be in her shop for a few minutes before he resumed his journey, but she wanted Celebrations to look its best.

It wasn't difficult to keep everything shipshape. Her only two customers that morning had each made significant purchases. The day was off to a good start from a revenue perspective, but each one had made their selections quickly and time dragged. Judy always hated not being busy, but today was worse than ever.

She checked her watch for the hundredth time. It wasn't even noon yet. She stepped behind the counter and straight-

NO MATTER HOW FAR

ened the stash of shopping bags stored there, ready to be put into service.

The lunch hour brought a steady stream of people making minor purchases—greeting cards and small gift items. Everyone remarked on the exquisite wooden ornaments on the tree in the window. After explaining, over and over, that they were family heirlooms and not for sale, she made a sign that read, "Ornaments for Display Only," and positioned it by the tree.

Her phone pinged again as she was trying to extricate herself from the display without knocking anything over. She hoped it would be Jeff, telling her that he'd arrived in Westbury.

Judy cursed under her breath as she knocked over a ceramic squirrel. She'd come back to straighten it up—she wanted to read that message.

Flat tire has delayed me by about 3 hours. Picked up a nail somewhere. I'm getting a new tire and will be on my way shortly. I should be there before you close. Is this still convenient for you?

Of course! Judy texted back. *Don't worry if you're going to be later. I don't have plans tonight. I'll wait for you. Just drive safely.*

Will do and thank you! See you soon!!

Judy blew out a deep breath. At least he was still coming. She shook her head. What was going on with her? A man she barely knew was stopping by to pick up a package. The butterflies in her stomach made no sense. She needed to get hold of herself.

The afternoon had, mercifully, been busy. It was almost closing time when Judy was wrapping a set of ceramic woodland creatures in heavy white paper and chatting with the customer.

The bell to the shop tinkled.

Judy glanced up. There, framed in the doorway, stood a tall, solidly built man with a full head of salt-and-pepper hair. He was the sort of man who would have been attractive when young but whose looks had matured into rugged handsomeness.

His eyes met hers, and a smile made his face shine. He stepped inside and ambled toward Judy, waiting while she finished the transaction with her customer.

Judy wrapped the items as fast as she could and double-bagged them in a sturdy shopping bag. She passed the purchase across the counter to the customer, thanking her for coming in.

The woman nodded to Jeff as she made her way out of the shop.

Judy and Jeff smiled at each other across the counter.

"You made it!" Judy said. "I was so sorry to hear about your tire."

"These things happen. At least it didn't cause an accident. I made good time once I was back on the road."

"I'm glad." Judy brushed a strand of her strawberry blonde hair off of her forehead. "Let me get you what you came all this way for." She went into the storage room and returned with the box. She placed it on the counter in front of him and walked to the door, engaging the lock and turning the sign to Closed.

Jeff opened the flaps and read one of the tags.

Judy busied herself with a display on a round table by the door.

After examining another ornament and reading the tag, Jeff turned to her. "I can't tell you how much this means to me. I know it sounds crazy—I barely knew my uncle, and I certainly didn't know about these ornaments—but it's like you've given me back part of my history."

Judy came to stand next to him. "I can understand that. It makes me so happy to hear you say this." She pointed to the display window. "Did you see the ones I have?"

He shook his head. "I was in such a hurry to see you that I didn't pay any attention to your window. I'm sorry."

Judy smiled at him. "Let's go look. I think I have a set that's nearly identical to yours." She retrieved her coat from the backroom and led him onto the sidewalk. Dusk was falling, and the shop was in deep shade from the tall trees lining the square. The window display shone brightly, and the small tree with the ornaments took center stage.

They stood, side by side, as Jeff leaned forward and studied every ornament. "They're magnificent," he said, his voice hoarse. "Do you display them like this every year?"

"No. I just put these decorations up last night. I got a sudden brain wave that you might like to see them displayed on a tree."

Jeff turned to her. "I love it. Thank you so much for doing this!"

"It was my pleasure. I had fun with it, and everyone who walks by will enjoy the ornaments, too." She shifted from one foot to the other. "I guess I'd better let you get on your way. You have a long way to go if you want to make up the three hours you lost."

"I got a motel room at a place along the highway," he said. "Eight hours of driving in one day is enough for me. I'll get a good night's sleep and set out again tomorrow." He faced her. "I was hoping you'd join me for dinner, actually. Unless you have other plans—I know this is very last minute. I'd love to thank you," he pointed to the window, "for all of this."

"I'd like that," she said.

"I passed a good-looking place not far from here," he said. "Stuart's Steakhouse. Is it any good—or is there somewhere else you'd enjoy?"

"Stuart's is wonderful but a bit pricey," Judy said.

Jeff made a dismissive gesture with his hand. "Don't worry about that. A nice meal is the very least I can do for you."

They stowed his box of ornaments on the floor of his backseat. Jeff opened the car door for her, and they were on their way.

~

THE WAITER STEPPED up to their table and cleared his throat. Jeff paused mid-sentence to look up.

"Will there be anything else, sir?"

"No, thank you. I've signed the credit card slip." Jeff pointed to the small black tray at the end of the table.

Judy looked at her watch and gasped. "It's MIDNIGHT."

They both looked around the restaurant and noticed that they were the only patrons still there.

"I'm so sorry," Jeff said to the waiter. "We ... we lost all track of time." Jeff pulled another twenty out of his wallet and placed it on the tray.

Judy snatched her coat off the back of her chair and clutched it to her chest.

"It looked like you were having a wonderful time," the man said. "I hated to disturb you."

"Thank you—and Merry Christmas," Jeff said as he and Judy made a hasty exit.

They turned to each other as the door shut behind them and burst out laughing.

"I can't remember the last time I closed a place down," Judy said.

Jeff took her coat and held it out for her. "Neither can I. He was right—I was having a wonderful time."

Judy felt herself flush.

"I'd better get you back to Celebrations. You have to work tomorrow."

"I walked to work this morning—I always do that when the weather permits. Would you mind dropping me off at my house?"

"Of course not."

They got into Jeff's car and he began driving.

"Actually—we can swing by the Olsson house on the way. The electricity isn't on yet, or I'd give you a tour. At least you can see the outside."

"I'd like that—especially after the remarkable story you just told me about how you acquired title to it."

"I still can't believe it, myself. Sometimes I wonder if I've lost my mind." She pointed ahead of them. "Turn left here, and then it's the fifth house on the right."

Jeff slowed the car and pulled to a stop at the curb. "Holy cow," he murmured.

"Let's get out. You can see it so much better."

"Are you sure? It's so late …"

Judy opened her car door, and he followed suit.

The moon shone brightly in the cloudless sky.

Jeff tilted his head back and examined the ornate façade. "What a glorious specimen of Victorian architecture," he finally said.

"It's handsome, isn't it? I've loved this house my whole life."

"Magnificent." Jeff looked at her. "You shouldn't have any second thoughts about buying this place. I don't know how anyone could resist. I love the idea that my box of ornaments was hidden away in that attic. I'm going to come by tomorrow, on my way out of town, to take a picture of it."

"Would you like to see the inside?"

"Yes … but I can't ask you to get up early to show it to me before you open Celebrations. It's way past midnight, as it is."

"If you're going to drive all day tomorrow, you'll need to sleep in," Judy said. "My handyman is going to be at the house tomorrow morning, waiting for the electrical company inspector to approve the new panel and give the go-ahead to turn the power back on. Sam will be more than happy to give you a tour. He's as excited about this place as I am."

"If you really don't mind? I definitely want to see inside."

"Consider it done. I'll text Sam first thing in the morning."

"And now, I'd better get you home." Jeff turned back to the car.

"I'm four houses down, on the other side of the street. I can walk."

Jeff joined her on the sidewalk.

"It's a safe neighborhood," Judy said. "You don't have to walk me home."

"I *want* to walk you home," he said.

They continued in silence. When they reached Judy's house, she fumbled for her key and unlocked her door.

"Thank you," they both started to say at the same time.

Jeff smiled down at her.

"I enjoyed dinner very much. You certainly didn't have to do that."

"This has been the best day I've had in years," Jeff said. "I'm grateful that your kind heart led you to find the owner of those ornaments, but I'm most thankful that they led me to you." He leaned down and kissed her on the cheek. "I'll come by Celebrations tomorrow morning before I head out."

"I'll look forward to it," Judy said breathlessly. "Good night, Jeff."

CHAPTER 14

*J*eff pulled in behind the pickup truck parked at the curb. He'd tossed and turned all night, replaying the evening in his mind. At six-thirty, he'd finally gotten up, showered, and had breakfast before driving to the house at eight.

He was heading up the walkway to the house when Sam opened the front door. Slim and agile, Sam looked to be a few years older than Jeff. His firm grip when they shook hands attested to the fact that Sam worked hard with his hands.

"You must be Jeff Carson. I'm Sam Torres."

"Judy said that you wouldn't mind giving me a tour of the house. I know you're working—I don't want to get in your way."

"Not at all," Sam assured him. "Come on in. Judy said you studied architecture. I'll bet you can tell me some things about this place. Follow me ..."

The two men made their way through every room on the first floor, their pace slowing as they discussed maintenance issues and needed repairs. By the time they reached the second floor, they were lost in detailed discussions of restoration techniques and replacement options.

"You really know your stuff," Sam said, taking a small spiral-bound notebook out of his pocket and jotting down notes.

"I guess owning a hardware store and fixing up my own house taught me a few things."

"Sure," Sam said, "but don't sell yourself short. You're quite the expert."

"That's some compliment, coming from you," Jeff said. "Thank you."

They came to the flight of stairs leading to the turret room.

"Let me show you the attic, where Judy found that box of ornaments," Sam said, leading the way up the stairs.

Jeff stepped into the turret room and was immediately drawn to the windows. "Look at this view!" he said. "There's no real purpose for this room other than to admire the scenery." He shook his head. "They don't build 'em like this anymore."

"You can say that again," Sam replied.

Jeff turned to Sam. "Judy's got a lot on her plate with this one."

"She sure has."

"Have you ever done any fix and flips of your own?"

"I'm too busy with my regular handyman customers. Fixing and flipping is too much work for an old guy like me."

"I don't think there's anything a younger man could do that you can't, but I understand not wanting to take on an entire house on your own. I thought about buying a little fixer-upper in my old neighborhood, but it just wouldn't be the same without Millie to help me with paint colors and wallpaper and ..." Jeff turned to the window and spoke to Sam's reflection. He didn't want the man to see the tears starting to form.

"Millie ... my wife ... she's been gone for three years now." Jeff's voice was quiet. "I took this trip to make a new start, but sometimes I'm not sure if I did the right thing."

Sam nodded slowly. One of his innate abilities was knowing when someone needed to talk.

"All I know is that keeping everything the same—following all my old routines—was holding me back."

Sam leaned against the door frame.

"I sold that house, the one Millie and I fixed up. We bought it right after we married—it was all we could afford then." Jeff smiled. "I loved that place, but it didn't feel like home anymore. I'd planned to buy another one, near my son and daughter-in-law, but that didn't feel right, either. I was still in the same town, following the same patterns, living a life that didn't exist anymore." Jeff turned back to Sam. "That's when I realized I needed to get away."

"It's good to listen to your gut," Sam said. "You can try to ignore it, but your longing and discontent will always remain. Best to deal with it."

"Exactly. That's why I'm headed to Phoenix for the holidays, I need to start new traditions. I want to enjoy Christmas again."

"It can be a magical time of year. At least in Westbury. If you weren't leaving this afternoon, I'd tell you to drive up the hill to see the Christmas lights at Rose—"

A loud knock on the front door interrupted him.

"That must be the inspector from the electric company," Sam said. He moved to the top of the stairs. "Your box was found in the attic—through that door, over there." He pointed to the attic door. "Have a look around. I'll be out back with the inspector."

"Thanks," Jeff said.

"Take your time," Sam said, his voice trailing off as he headed down the stairs.

Jeff entered the dim interior of the attic. He engaged the flashlight on his phone and trained it around the room. The boxes stacked against the wall were labeled in the precise lettering that he now recognized as his uncle's. It was odd, he mused, that the detritus of a lifetime could give him clues about the reclusive man. The attic was as neat and orderly as the ornaments William had carved.

Jeff backed out of the space and stepped onto the stairs. The railing was pulling away from the wall and the top step had too much give in it. He should mention both to Sam. Jeff opened the notes app on his phone and recorded his findings.

Jeff made another pass through the second floor, examining every doorframe, floorboard, fireplace, and plumbing fixture. His fingers tapped away at the screen of his phone, making notes. He was in the parlor at the front of the house when Sam found him.

"Jeff?"

Jeff was squatting in front of the fireplace, craning his neck to see up the chimney. "You'll need a chimney sweep in here before any of these fireplaces can be used," he said, "but I'm sure you know that."

"I thought you would have left hours ago. Aren't you driving to Phoenix for Christmas?"

"Yes. I took another look around. I found some stuff and made notes for you. I thought I'd tell you about them and be on my way."

Sam looked at him. "Do you know what time it is?

"I was making notes on my phone, and the last time I paid attention to the time, it was just after noon." Jeff checked the time on his phone now. His eyebrows shot up.

"It's almost dinnertime," Sam said. "I should have come looking for you. I've been wrangling with the electrical guy this entire time. He didn't think we'd done the work up to code. Well ... we did! I finally insisted he get his supervisor on the line so we could work it all out."

"Are they turning the power back on?"

Sam nodded, smiling. "First thing tomorrow morning."

"Good work," Jeff said, coming to Sam and clapping him on the back.

"Anyway, I'd better quit talking and let you get on your way. Tomorrow's Christmas Eve. You've got a lot of driving ahead of you."

Jeff pursed his lips, thinking. "I'm not going to leave tonight. If I get started early tomorrow, I can still be there on the afternoon of Christmas Day."

"In that case," Sam said, "would you like to come for dinner at my house tonight? I'd love for you to meet Joan."

"Joan must be a very gracious woman if she doesn't mind you bringing a stranger home for dinner." He raised a hand to stop Sam from protesting. "I've got another plan for myself. Before we head out, can we go over the notes I've made about the house?"

"Of course," Sam said. "I'd be glad to get your input."

Jeff tapped on the screen of his phone and began scrolling. He looked over the top of his glasses at Sam. "Remember—this is free advice, so it's worth what you paid for it." He began working his way through his list as Sam pulled out his notebook and pencil.

～

JUDY WAS TURNING the sign to Closed when she recognized the figure walking toward her shop. She blinked twice. She'd spent the day wishing she'd see Jeff again. Was she imagining this? His warm smile as she opened the door to him told her that he was really there.

"I'm like a bad penny," he said. "I keep turning up. At dinnertime, no less."

"I'm delighted to see you." Judy drew him inside the shop. "Why are you still here? You should be at least four hundred miles south of Westbury by now."

"I spent the day at your new house—which is more magnificent than I first thought—and wanted to let you know what we came up with."

"We?"

"Sam and me. You've had a couple of old-house buffs combing through the place together. No wonder I lost track of time."

"So, the two of you know what needs to be done?"

Jeff nodded. "I was hoping to entice you to have dinner with me again, and I'll tell you all about it."

Judy grinned at him. "You know I can't say no to this. But I do have one condition."

"Name it."

"You let me buy."

"No … I'm inviting you."

"Then I'm afraid you're out of luck," Judy folded her arms across her chest.

Jeff gave an exaggerated sigh. "All right—if you're going to play hardball with me."

"I know just where I want to take you," Judy said, grabbing her purse and coat. "Pete's Bistro—right across the square."

"Lead the way, madam," Jeff said.

Pete greeted Judy warmly, raising an eyebrow at her behind Jeff's back.

Judy blushed.

"This has the feel of a place that all the locals love," Jeff observed as they slipped into a booth.

"It certainly is. Pete's daily specials are always terrific, and his wife, Laura, owns the bakery next door. Her pie of the day is legendary. I don't even have to look at the menu—today's are meatloaf and apple pie."

Jeff closed his menu. "Say no more. That's what I'll have."

As soon as the waiter brought Jeff a cup of coffee and Judy an iced tea, she turned to Jeff. "I'm on pins and needles. Please tell me what you think of the place."

Jeff consulted the notes on his phone and began. Judy interrupted him with questions as they made their way through the meal. By the time their pieces of pie were placed in front of them, Judy was choking back tears.

"New sewer lines, a new roof, upgrades to all the plumbing lines and fixtures, and a new kitchen are all mandatory? That doesn't include cosmetic upgrades? I'm afraid to ask, but I have to know. How much will all this set me back?"

"Remember—you bought the place for less than the value of the lot. These things will cost less than building a new house."

"That isn't reassuring," she said. "Just tell me."

Jeff inhaled slowly. "This is just a guess—the number could vary greatly, based upon what you find when you get started … and on the finishes you choose …"

"The number?" Judy grabbed his elbow.

"Two to three hundred—more like three."

"THOUSAND?"

He nodded.

Judy put her elbows on the table and rested her face in her

hands, moaning softly. "I … cannot … afford that." She choked on the words. "Not anything close to that. Oh my God—what have I done?"

"It's not as bad as all that, is it?"

She tilted her head to look at him. "I don't even want to live in the place. I got carried away at the tax sale because some stupid developer was bidding on it. My attorney said he'd tear it down and put up a whole bunch of houses." She sniffled. "Probably some hideous modern things that would stick out like sore thumbs." She began to cry. "I couldn't let that happen, could I?"

"Of course not," Jeff said.

"But now that's what's going to happen because I can't afford to do all of this."

"You could fix it up and sell it," Jeff suggested.

"That's what I planned to do, but not if I had to put that much into it. I'll have to take out a big loan to do the work, and what if it doesn't sell? I don't think I want to take that risk—I'll need to sell my position to that damned developer."

"You don't have to decide this right now," Jeff said. "Why don't you think about it?"

"I suppose you're right," Judy said.

"I didn't mean to upset you with all of this," Jeff said as they walked across the square, headed to her house.

Judy took a deep breath. "I know you didn't. I'm grateful that you spent so much time looking at the place and shared your expertise with me." The chilly night air was clearing her head. "This is my problem, and I'll get myself out of it. All you need to worry about is making your way to Phoenix in time for Christmas dinner."

They reached her front door, and Jeff turned her to him. "Thank you for dinner. I'm sorry that our conversation wasn't as fun as last night's. Try not to let this spoil your holiday. Things may look different in the morning."

"I'll hold that thought," she said. "You're a kind man, Jeff Carson, and I'm so glad I met you." She leaned into him, aiming for his cheek.

Jeff turned his face, and their lips met in a brief kiss.

"Merry Christmas, Judy. I hope the coming year brings you happiness."

CHAPTER 15

*J*udy smiled at the next person waiting in line at the register as she tucked a receipt in a shopping bag and handed it to the woman standing in front of her. "Thank you and Merry Christmas," she said.

Celebrations had been slammed with shoppers since the moment she'd unlocked the door. Christmas Eve was always a busy day, but Judy sensed that this might be her best one yet. The average sale was higher than usual, and her candles and bath products were flying off the shelves. She'd have to reorder the most popular items next week. Still, she doubted the extra holiday revenue would make much of a dent in the repair costs she and Jeff went over last night at dinner.

She should be giddy with excitement over the day's mounting sales, she told herself. Instead, she was crestfallen that she hadn't heard anything more from Jeff—not even a text that he was on his way to Phoenix. She kept her cell phone in a drawer by the register and checked for messages when she had the chance. There was nothing from him. She'd probably put him off with her emotional outburst the prior evening.

Judy forced a smile and continued answering customer questions and ringing up sales. By the time she closed the shop at three o'clock—early, because it was Christmas Eve—she was exhausted. She glanced around the usually neat and orderly space. Her displays were in complete disarray, with bare shelves and items discarded by shoppers on the nearest available surface. She really should spend an hour or two tidying things up, but she was too tired. She didn't have to be anywhere on Christmas Day until the late afternoon when she'd attend the annual potluck dinner at Rosemont. She'd start her Crock-Pot macaroni and cheese and make the crustless cranberry pie that she took to the potluck every year when she got home from church that night and spend Christmas morning restoring order to Celebrations.

Judy got her coat and purse and headed for the door. She was just turning the key in the lock when she remembered her phone, sitting in the drawer. She went back inside, and when she opened the drawer, her heart leaped into her throat. She had a text message from Jeff.

Please stop by the Olsson house on your way home from Celebrations.

Judy felt her smile from her toes to the tips of her ears. He must have left a surprise for her on his way out of town. She quickened her pace as she got closer to the house. What could it be? A poinsettia? She decided that was the most likely thing. He could have bought one almost anywhere and left it on the front porch.

She was almost jogging as she turned the corner and approached the Olsson house. She pushed open the rickety iron gate and stepped onto the walkway, coming to a halt when she saw what was waiting for her.

Jeff was standing at the top of the steps. Behind him was a live Christmas tree, strung with lights and decorated with his ornaments. The railings on either side of the steps were festooned with pine garlands. A wreath with holly berries hung on the front door. Candles trailed up the steps, their flames flickering in the breeze. At his feet stood a large wicker hamper. A red-and-green plaid throw was draped over the hamper, and a champagne bottle perched on top, flanked by two flutes.

Judy brought her hand to her heart. "You're … you're here."

Jeff came down the steps to meet her. "I did a lot of thinking last night," he said as he drew her into his arms, "about what I want for the next chapter of my life."

"Oh?" She tilted her head back to look into his eyes.

"I couldn't go to Phoenix without talking to you first." He glanced at his handiwork on the porch. "I planned to wait until after we'd eaten our picnic and drunk our champagne, but I'm just going to go for it. Do you believe in love at first sight?"

Her eyes grew moist.

Jeff pressed on. "I always thought that was the most ridiculous concept. Pure Hollywood. Until I met you. I know we've only just met, but at a certain point in life, you know when you know. You're the one for me—the one I want to live out the rest of my days with. We clicked—like we'd known each other our whole lives—that first night on the phone. I think you feel it, too?"

She nodded, unable to find her voice.

"I'm not asking you to decide right now. I can appreciate that you might need more time, but would you entertain the idea of having me in your life?"

Judy grasped his hands and brought them to her heart. "I feel the same way you do, Jeff. I think I could be happy spending the rest of my life with you."

Jeff pulled her against him, and they kissed until the chill in the air didn't reach them and the loneliness of the years melted away.

JUDY SPREAD another smear of brie onto a sea salt and rosemary cracker and popped it into her mouth. She and Jeff were sitting on the plaid throw spread out in front of the fireplace in the parlor. They'd brought the candles inside with them, and Judy had arranged them on the hearth. The decorated tree stood in the center of the room, its battery-operated lights twinkling cheerily.

She took a sip of champagne and pointed to the array of treats from the hamper that now lay spread out around them. "Where did you find all this?"

Jeff looked genuinely pleased with himself. "The desk clerk at my motel told me to call a place outside of town called The Mill. I'm sure you know it?"

Judy nodded. "That would be the place to go for this sort of spread. I'm impressed," she said, snuggling against him. "Look at this. My first Christmas in this house." She sighed heavily. "It'll be my only Christmas in the house."

"Have you decided what you're going to do with it?" His body tensed.

"I've got to sell it. As much as I hate to, I don't have the money to restore it. I only hope that someone will be interested in it—other than that hideous developer."

Jeff wrapped an arm around her and nodded.

They stared at the flickering candles. Wax dripped, making a soft thud on the slate. In the distance, somewhere on the square, carolers were singing.

Judy suddenly popped up and turned to look at Jeff. "You should take the house!"

"What?"

"I'll bet Alma was the one paying the taxes, all those years after William died. This should be *your* house."

"There's no way to know that, Judy," Jeff said. "My dad left her well off, so she would have had the money to pay them, but her financial records were like the rest of her life—a complete mess. She didn't trust banks and kept money under her mattress. Anything she couldn't pay in cash she got a money order or cashier's check for. I won't take it from you, Judy."

She felt her cheeks flush. It probably sounded like she was trying to pass the buck. She didn't know whether Jeff could afford the repairs. What if he thought she was trying to dump it all on him?

She turned away and rubbed at the back of her neck. "Never mind. I don't know what I was thinking. I'm just getting desperate, you know? The thought of this house being torn down, a part of my past—both our pasts—I just feel helpless."

He pulled back and scooted around to face her. "Judy, I won't take it from you."

"Yes." She looked down. Why was he repeating himself?

"But," he said, nudging her chin. "I'll buy it from you."

Her head snapped up. "No! That's not what I meant. I don't want you to buy it."

"Okay." Jeff held up his hands. "You got it. You're the legal owner. You can sell it to whoever you want."

Judy didn't know what to say.

"Who do you want, Judy?"

Without thinking she answered, "I want you—"

He grinned and drew her in for a deep kiss. "I want you too, Judy."

When they pulled apart, she said, "—to have this house, Jeff. I want you to have this house." She laughed and then she kissed him again.

"I've never done business this way." He smiled down at her. "I should buy houses more often."

Judy pushed him playfully on the chest. "I'm giving you the house. Think of it as an early Christmas present."

"I already have my Christmas present—I'm holding you in my arms."

Judy rolled her eyes and laughed. "You're cheesier than that charcuterie board."

"Ouch."

"I'm serious, Jeff."

"And I'm serious when I say that I want to buy this house. At full appraised price."

"I can't let you do that. That's more than I've invested in it."

"Okay, tell you what, I'll cover your investment, plus interest—"

She started to protest but he held a finger to her lips to shush her.

"—and I'll pay Sam's repair fees. I'd like to keep him on to help me with the house."

Judy sighed. "I'm not going to convince you otherwise, am I?"

"Nope. I do have a buyer's closing condition, though"

"And that is?"

"Promise me you'll help me decorate for Christmas next year. I had a hell of a time tracking down these decorations."

Judy laughed and held out her hand. "Deal."

They shook on it.

"I guess I'll have my attorney Susan draw up the paperwork then."

"Perfect."

Judy yawned and stretched.

"Are you still headed to Phoenix tomorrow?"

"I called my cousin and told him I'd been delayed—that I thought I'd still come out for a week in January and that I might bring someone with me."

Judy grinned. "Is that an invitation?"

"It most certainly is."

"Then I accept. Seems like you're making all my dreams come true." Judy pulled him to her and kissed him. "As for tomorrow, will you come with me to Rosemont for dinner?"

"I have no idea what or where that is, but I'd be delighted if it wouldn't be an imposition on anyone to have a last-minute plus one."

"Not at all. Christmas dinner at Rosemont is the most wonderful tradition. All my friends go. You can meet Susan, and Sam and his wife will be there. You'll love the house, too."

"I'm anxious to talk to Sam—I hope he'll stay on to help me with the renovations."

"He'll be thrilled. He's done a lot of work at Rosemont, too. It's the huge stone manor home on the hill overlooking town. One of my best friends, Maggie Martin and her husband, own it. Wait until you hear how *she* acquired the house …"

Jeff propped his head on his elbow and watched the candlelight play across Judy's face as she filled him in on the facts and fictions of his new hometown. The sun had set by the time she'd finished her tale and shadows hovered in the corners of the parlor.

Judy shivered and Jeff got to his feet, offering his hand to help her up.

"I haven't turned the heat on yet," Judy said. "I wanted to get the furnaces thoroughly checked before I did."

"That makes sense," Jeff said, picking up the throw as Judy began to pack the remnants of their snacks into the hamper.

A sound from the foyer caught their attention.

"Did you hear something?" he asked.

She nodded and held up her hand as she listened. The room remained silent. "Must have been the wind," she said, bending back to the hamper.

The sound came again, this time more insistent.

"Someone's at the door," Jeff said. He grabbed one of the candles from the hearth and made his way to the door.

"It sounds like they're scratching at it," Judy said, following close behind. "Maybe we shouldn't open it."

Jeff put his hand on the inside door handle and two short barks erupted from the other side, followed by pitiful whimpering.

Jeff and Judy looked at each other.

"It's a dog!" he cried, throwing the door open.

A squirming mass of matted gray and white fur hurtled through the opening and ran laps around the foyer, coming to a sloppy stop at Jeff's feet.

Jeff squatted to examine the animal.

The dog leapt into his arms, covering Jeff's neck and chin with kisses.

He stood, clutching the dog to his chest. "There, there," he cooed. "Calm down. You're safe now."

Judy put her hand on the dog's back. "I'm not sure what kind of dog he is, but he's sure sweet."

"I'd say that there's some miniature schnauzer in there,

somewhere. His fur is so matted and dirty it's hard to get a good look at him."

"What should we do with him? The shelters will be closed on Christmas Eve."

Jeff held the dog away from himself and looked into the animal's pleading brown eyes. "I'd like to see if we can find his owner, but if we can't, I intend to keep him." He looked at Judy. "Do you like dogs?"

"I've always had cats, but I'm making room for all kinds of new things in my life." She winked at Jeff.

Jeff grinned. "I feel like a kid who's gotten a puppy for Christmas."

"I think that's exactly what's happened. What will you call him?"

Jeff pursed his lips. "I think 'Jolly' is a good name, given the time of year."

Judy laughed. "I agree. I'll keep him at my house tonight. I've got hamburger in the fridge. I can cook that for him—with some rice."

Jeff tucked the dog under his arm. "By the looks of him, he hasn't had a decent meal in a long time."

"It'll be a Christmas treat for him," Judy said. "Let's leave the hamper here for now. I think we need to take care of this guy right away."

"You're a kind woman, Judy," Jeff said.

Judy extinguished the candles and they stepped onto the porch.

"Maggie's husband—John Allen—is the local vet. You'll meet him at Rosemont tomorrow." She locked the front door.

"I'll make an appointment for Jolly as soon as possible."

"The way you've acquired this guy," she pointed to Jolly,

"reminds me of how Maggie found her dog—Eve—on her first night at Rosemont."

"Oh?"

They walked to Jeff's car; the now-contented creature nestled between them.

"There must be something about big houses and stray dogs here in Westbury. Wait until you hear the story ..."

CHAPTER 16

*J*oan Torres reached around Maggie to set her au gratin potato casserole on the buffet in the dining room. The tangy aroma of a glazed ham rose from the platter that Maggie had just put into place. Snippets of conversation and excited greetings swirled around them.

"It all looks lovely, as usual," Joan said, casting her glance over the dishes on the buffet.

"The Christmas potluck is my favorite holiday tradition," Maggie replied.

"How many do you expect this year?" Joan asked.

"Twenty-nine." Maggie and Joan turned to the arched entrance to the dining room where Judy—and Jeff—had just stepped into view.

"Make that thirty," Maggie said, training a quizzical glance on Joan. "Is that the guy with the ornament?"

Joan scanned the crowded room for her husband. Their eyes met, and she raised an eyebrow. He nodded back at her.

"I believe it is," Joan said, her tone rising with excitement.

"Sam liked the guy and told me he thought he and Judy would be perfect together."

"Your husband said that? Mr. Don't-Stick-Your-Nose-In-Other-People's-Business?"

"I know! So unusual for him. But that's what he said."

"They look like they go together, don't they?"

"Absolutely. Oh, I do hope this turns out well for Judy. She deserves to be with someone who'll appreciate her," Joan said.

"Maybe we'll witness another Christmas miracle here at Rosemont," Maggie whispered.

"I hate to interrupt you two," Marc Benson said as he stepped between them and reached for the spoon to scoop up a helping of potatoes. "I want to eat before I have to start playing the piano for the sing- along."

Guests continued to arrive, and the good cheer—and noise level—rose as the guests enjoyed the meal and got themselves caught up on each other's lives.

Jeff and Sam tucked themselves off to one side and were animatedly discussing the Olsson house renovations.

Joan sidled up to Judy. "He's staying, isn't he?"

Judy's eyes telegraphed her happiness as she nodded. "It's the most wonderful thing—I can't wait to tell you."

"And I can't wait to hear every detail." Joan put an arm around her friend's shoulder. "There's too much commotion here. Why don't you meet Maggie and me for lunch tomorrow? You can tell us all about it."

"I'd love that. Pete's at noon?"

"Where else?"

Alex Scanlon, Susan's brother-in-law and Maggie's successor as Mayor of Westbury, stood and tapped his water glass with his knife. The room quieted down. "All right, every-body. You know the drill. We all clean up and then head to the piano where our own Marc Benson," he smiled at his partner, "will lead us in a rousing session of carol singing."

The group leaped to their feet and began gathering dirty dishes and cutlery, cleaning the dining room with the precision of a circus breaking camp. When the dishwasher had been started, and the last pan had been dried and put away, they all assembled at the piano.

Marc sat on the bench and began warming up when John Allen stopped him. He gestured to Sam, who started handing out glasses of champagne. "As your local veterinarian, I'm not known for making speeches. I normally leave that to my wife," he said, nodding at Maggie, "or to Alex, our current mayor. But I'm making an exception tonight, so we can all welcome Westbury's newest resident." He motioned for Jeff to stand up. "If you haven't already introduced yourself to Jeff Carson, please do. He's purchasing the Olsson house and, from what I overheard a few minutes ago, plans to restore it to its former glory. As a native of Westbury, I'm thrilled to see our historic treasures honored and protected. So—please raise your glasses and join me in giving Jeff a hearty welcome to Westbury!"

Jeff turned quizzical eyes to Judy.

She shrugged and shook her head, then stretched up and kissed him.

Accompanied by a chorus of "hear, hear" and a burst of applause, the group toasted their new friend.

Joan slipped into the crowd next to Maggie and put her arm around her friend's waist. "We've definitely got ourselves another Christmas miracle."

THE END

IF YOU ENJOYED *No Matter How Far*, you'll want to catch up with Maggie, John, Judy, and the rest of the cast (both two and four-legged) in the Rosemont series. If you love romance with a dash of mystery/thriller/suspense, here's the bestselling book where it all began—*Coming to Rosemont.*

Thank You for Reading!

If you enjoyed *No Matter How Far*, I'd be grateful if you wrote a review.

Just a few lines on Amazon or Goodreads would be great. Reviews are the best gift an author can receive. They encourage us when they're good, help us improve our next book when they're not, and help other readers make informed choices when purchasing books. Goodreads reviews help readers find new books. Reviews on Amazon keep the Amazon algorithms humming and are the most helpful aide in selling books! Thank you.

To post a review on Amazon:

1. Go to the product detail page for *No Matter How Far* on Amazon.com.

2. Click "Write a customer review" in the Customer Reviews section.

3. Write your review and click Submit.

In gratitude,
Barbara Hinske

JUST FOR YOU!

Wonder what Maggie was thinking when the book ended? Exclusively for readers who finished *No Matter How Far,* take a look at Maggie's Diary Entry for that day at https://barbarahinske.com/maggies-diary.

ACKNOWLEDGMENTS

I'm blessed with the wisdom and support of many kind and generous people. I want to thank the most supportive and delightful group of champions an author could hope for:

My insightful and supportive assistant Lisa Coleman who keeps all the plates spinning;

My life coach Mat Boggs for your wisdom and guidance;

My kind and generous legal team, Kenneth Kleinberg, Esq., and Michael McCarthy—thank you for believing in my vision;

The professional "dream team" of my editors Linden Gross, Jesika St. Clair, and proofreader Dana Lee;

Elizabeth Mackey for a beautiful cover.

ACKNOWLEDGMENTS

Recurring Characters

ACOSTA

Grace: older sister to Tommy; David Wheeler's high school sweetheart; plans to attend Highpointe College upon graduation; babysits for the Scanlons

Iris: mother to Grace and Tommy with husband, Kevin

Kevin: professor at Highpointe College

Tommy: became friends with Nicole Nash and David Wheeler while an in-patient at Mercy Hospital

Alistair: butler at Rosemont for over fifty years, now a friendly ghost who lives in the attic

John Allen: veterinarian and owner of Westbury Animal Hospital, Maggie Martin's husband, adopted grandfather to baby Julia and twins Sophie and Sarah

Anita Archer: owner of Archer's Bridal

Kevin Baxter: member of Highpointe College Board of Trustees

Marc Benson: partner of Alex Scanlon, musician

Nigel Blythe: owner of Blythe Rare Books in London, bought books stolen from Highpointe College Library, poisoned Hazel Harrington, attempted to kill Sunday Sloan and Anthony Plume

Harriet and Larry Burman: owners of Burman Jewelers

Jeff Carson: Widower; former wife, Millie, died 3 years ago; son Jason and daughter-in-law Sharon; grandchildren Tyler and Talia; cares about animal shelter; mother, Alma, uncle, William Olsson

Charlotte: owner of Candy Alley Candy Shop

DELGADO BROTHERS: involved in scheme to embezzle money from the Westbury Town Workers' Pension Fund

Chuck: former Westbury town councilmember; owner of D's Liquor and Convenience Store

Ron: investment advisor and CPA; married to William Wheeler's sister

FITZPATRICK

Laura: owner of Laura's Bakery; mother of one with husband, Pete

Pete: owner of Pete's Bistro, a popular lunch spot for Westbury town councilmembers

Gloria Harper: resident of Fairview Terraces, married to Glenn Vaughn, acts as surrogate grandmother to David Wheeler

Hazel Harrington: deceased rare-book librarian at Highpointe College, poisoned by Nigel Blythe

Robert Harris: rare-book librarian at Cambridge University, friend to Sunday Sloan

Frank Haynes: repentant crony of the Delgados, Westbury town councilmember, owner of Haynes Enterprises (holding company of fast food restaurants), founder and principal funder of Forever Friends dog rescue, grandson of Hector Martin, married to Loretta Nash

HOLMES

George: emcee of the annual Easter Carnival, father of three with wife, Tonya

Tonya: Westbury town councilmember; close friend of Maggie Martin

Russell Isaac: Westbury town councilmember, inherited auto parts business, former acting mayor of Westbury, involved in scheme to of Delgado brothers

Lyla Kershaw: works in accounting department at Highpointe College Library; close friend of Sunday Sloan; birth mother of Josh Newlon

Tim Knudsen: realtor, Westbury town councilmember, married to Nancy

Ian Lawry: former president of Highpointe College

MARTIN

Amy: Maggie Martin's daughter-in-law; mother to twins, Sophie and Sarah, with husband, Mike Martin

Hector and Silas: deceased town patriarchs; Silas (Hector's father) amassed a fortune from the local sawmill, real estate, and other ventures and built the Rosemont estate; Hector donated his rare book collection to Highpointe College and left his estate to his living heirs—grandnephew, Paul Martin, and grandson, Frank Haynes (Frank's father was Hector's illegitimate son)

Maggie: current owner of Rosemont and president of Highpointe College; widow of Paul Martin; former forensic accountant and mayor of Westbury; married to John Allen; mother to Mike Martin and Susan (Martin) Scanlon; grandmother to Julia Scanlon and twins, Sophie and Sarah Martin

Mike: Maggie Martin's adult son, lives in California with wife, Amy, and twin daughters, Sophie and Sarah

Paul: Maggie Martin's first husband, deceased; embezzled funds while president of Windsor College; father of Susan (Martin) Scanlon and Mike Martin; had an affair with Loretta Nash and fathered Nicole Nash

Sophie and Sarah: twin daughters of Amy and Mike Martin; close friends of Marissa Nash; Maggie Martin's granddaughter

Gordon Mortimer: antiques dealer and appraiser

NASH

Loretta: current financial analyst at Haynes Enterprises; married to Frank Haynes; mother to Marissa, Sean, and Nicole, with baby number four on the way; former mistress of Paul Martin

Marissa, Nicole, Sean: Loretta's children, adopted by stepfather, Frank Haynes; Marissa (oldest) babysits for the Scanlons and is friends with Maggie Martin's twin granddaughters; Nicole (youngest) received a kidney from Susan Scanlon after it was discovered that they had the same father, Paul Martin; Sean works as David Wheeler's apprentice at Forever Friends and the animal hospital

Josh Newlon: Maggie Martin's administrative assistant; Lyla Kershaw's birth son; Sunday Sloan's boyfriend

Juan: veterinary technician at Westbury Animal Hospital

Anthony Plume: professor and dean of English Literature at Highpointe College; stole rare books from the college library and sold them to Nigel Blythe

SCANLON

Aaron: orthopedic surgeon; married to Maggie's daughter, Susan; father to baby Julia; brother to Alex

Alex: attorney who succeeds Maggie Martin as mayor of Westbury; partner of Marc Benson

Julia: infant daughter of Susan and Aaron Scanlon; Maggie Martin's granddaughter

Susan (née Martin): Maggie Martin's adult daughter; attorney works at brother-in-law Alex's firm; helped Josh Newlon find his birth mother; nearly died donating kidney to stepsister, Nicole Nash

Sunday Sloan: rare-book librarian at Highpointe College; friend of Lyla Kershaw; Josh Newlon's girlfriend

Forest Smith: attorney at Stetson & Graham; assigned to assist Alex Scanlon; died in a suspicious fall off a bridge

Bill Stetson: partner at Stetson & Graham, Westbury's outside law firm

Chief Andrew (Andy) Thomas: Westbury's chief of police

Joan and Sam Torres: wife and husband; Maggie Martin's close friends, who befriended her on her first day in Westbury; Joan works as a police dispatcher, Sam as a handyman

Lyndon Upton: professor of finance at University of Chicago, former colleague of Maggie Martin's; volunteered to help with Westbury's embezzlement case

Glenn Vaughn: resident of Fairview Terraces; married to Gloria Harper; acts as surrogate grandfather to David Wheeler

WHEELER

David: works with therapy dogs; helps at Forever Friends and Westbury Animal Hospital; son of William and Jackie Wheeler; Grace Acosta's boyfriend

Jackie: wife of disgraced former mayor William Wheeler; mother to David

William: former mayor of Westbury convicted for fraud and embezzlement; committed suicide in prison; father to David and husband to Jackie

Judy Young: business-savvy owner of Celebrations Gift Shop and town gossip; close friend of Maggie Martin; maiden name Jorgenson

<u>*Westbury's Forever Friends*</u>

Blossom, Buttercup, and Bubbles: John Allen and Maggie Martin's cats, named after PowerPuff Girls

Cooper: the Scanlons' male golden retriever, a gift from David Wheeler to help baby Julia fall asleep

Daisy: Sean Nash's female Aussie-cattle dog mix

Dan: Josh Newlon's large black Labrador, who has a calming effect on baby Julia

Dodger: David Wheeler's constant companion, a mid-sized mutt with one eye, who works as a therapy dog at Fairview Terraces and Mercy Hospital

Eve: Maggie Martin's faithful terrier mix; found shivering in the snow, outside Rosemont, on Maggie's first night in Westbury

Jolly: Jeff Carson's schnauzer mix, adopted on Christmas Eve with Judy Young at the Olsson house

Magellan: Tommy Acosta's cat

Namor: David Wheeler's gray cat with four white paws; brother to Blossom, Buttercup, and Bubbles; was named after John Allen's dog, "Roman" spelled backwards

Roman: John Allen's gentle golden retriever

Rusty: Sam and Joan Torres's dog

Sally: Frank Haynes' overweight border collie mix

Snowball: Marissa and Nicole Nash's male terrier-schnauzer mix

ABOUT THE AUTHOR

USA Today Bestselling Author BARBARA HINSKE is an attorney and novelist. She's authored the Guiding Emily series, the mystery thriller collection "Who's There?", the Paws & Pastries series, two novellas in The Wishing Tree series, and the beloved *Rosemont Series*. Her novella *The Christmas Club* was made into a Hallmark Channel movie of the same name in 2019.

She is extremely grateful to her readers! She inherited the writing gene from her father who wrote mysteries when he retired and told her a story every night of her childhood. She and her husband share their own Rosemont with two adorable and spoiled dogs. The old house keeps her husband busy with repair projects and her happily decorating, entertaining, and gardening. She also spends a lot of time baking and—as a result —dieting.

Please enjoy this excerpt from **When Dreams There Be,** the ninth book in the Rosemont series by Barbara Hinske:

"Drive… around… to…" Loretta Haynes's words were cut off by her strangled scream.

"To the maternity entrance." David finished her sentence as he turned into the main entrance of Mercy Hospital. "There are signs directing me. We'll be there in a second." He glanced nervously over his shoulder at the woman in labor in his back seat.

Dodger, his faithful companion and trained therapy dog, sat calmly next to Loretta. He turned his soulful brown eyes to meet David's, as if to affirm that it was good they'd be at the delivery room soon.

Loretta sank against the seat back and panted. "Don't park—take me right to the door."

David nodded vigorously and brought his attention back to the road. He put on his left turn signal and pulled onto a circular driveway that took him to a double set of automatic glass doors. The sign above the doors read "Delivery Drop-Off."

He put the car into park and leapt out of the door almost before the car stopped moving. David was halfway to the rear passenger door when one set of double doors opened and a man in green scrubs approached the car, pushing a wheelchair.

"Will you need one of these?" he asked.

David nodded. "I think the babies are about to come out." He opened Loretta's door as she emitted another scream.

The man reached in and put his arm around Loretta's shoulders. He helped her slide from the car into the wheelchair. "How close are the contractions?"

Loretta opened her mouth to answer, then screamed again.

The man looked at David. "How long have they been this close together?"

"The entire way here. Maybe ten minutes." David swayed nervously. "She's having twins."

The man's eyebrows shot up, and he began pushing Loretta rapidly toward the entrance. "Go park and come inside," he called over his shoulder. "You can give the admitting clerk her information. We'll take a quick look, but I think she'll be headed directly to the delivery room."

David watched until the doors closed behind Loretta's wheelchair before he got into the car again. He patted the seat next to him and Dodger lunged across the center console to take his usual seat next to his master.

"I've got to go inside to give them information about Loretta." David stroked the dog's silky ears. "You'll have to stay in the car. It shouldn't take long." He checked the time on his dashboard clock. "Frank will be here soon."

David put the car in gear and followed the arrows directing him to Labor and Delivery Short Term Parking. He cracked the windows before exiting the car. "Be a good boy, Dodger. I know you're not used to being left alone in the car."

Dodger thumped his tail on the seat.

"I'll be back as soon as I can. You're going to be fine." David strode away from the car. He was halfway to his destination when he heard Dodger emit one sharp, quick bark. He ignored his dog and continued walking.

David entered through the glass doors that Loretta had, finding himself immersed in the typical chaos of a busy hospital maternity department. Men and women in scrubs crisscrossed in front of him, intent on their tasks. The waiting room on his left was filled with family members of all ages. He glanced to his right and found a row of desks with employees seated behind plexiglass shields. A sign above the desks read "Admitting Department. Please take a number."

David pulled a piece of paper from the machine and was looking for a place to sit when he heard his number being called on the overhead address system. He breathed a sigh of relief and went to the only open window in the Admitting Department.

The woman didn't look up at him as he sat down opposite her, on the other side of the shield. "What's your wife's name?"

"OH! No! It's not my wife."

The woman tore her eyes from her computer screen to look at him.

"It's my... she's my boss's wife. He wasn't home when she went into labor."

"Name?"

"David Wheeler."

The woman rolled her eyes. "The name of the woman who's in labor?"

Crimson spread from David's collar to the tips of his ears at his mistake. "Loretta Haynes."

"Date of birth?"

"I don't know."

The woman's hands were still, poised above her keyboard. "Address. Hers—not yours."

He gave the appropriate reply.

"Insurance?"

David shrugged. "I'm sure they have it, but I don't know anything about it."

"Does she have her purse with her?"

David shook his head. "I didn't know to grab it when I locked up the house. Her husband should be here any minute. He'll have all of that."

"If there's nothing else you can tell me, you should sit with her in the waiting room. Someone will be with you shortly."

"She's not there. They've already taken her back. Loretta's contractions weren't even a minute apart when we got here."

The woman removed her reading glasses and looked at him closely. "Are you that young man who visits here with his therapy dog?"

"I am."

"Everyone around here loves you and…"

"Dodger."

"Yes. That's the one. Thank you for doing that. You bring comfort to a lot of people in scary situations."

"We love our therapy work." David leaned toward the woman. "She's going to be all right, isn't she? She was screaming like her body was being ripped apart."

The woman's expression grew soft. "Of course she is. There's nothing unusual about that. We see it all day long. Don't worry."

"It's just that she's having twins."

"The staff here will take good care of her."

David was pushing back his chair to stand when he heard his name being called. He turned to see Frank Haynes striding toward him, with Marissa, Sean, and Nicole trailing behind.

"Where is she?" Frank asked.

The woman behind the window tapped on her keyboard and consulted her computer screen. "You're Loretta Haynes's husband?"

Frank nodded.

"They've just put her in a delivery room. Would you like to be with her?"

"Yes!"

"I'll have a nurse get you outfitted. Do you have your insurance card?"

Frank shoved his hand in his pocket and withdrew his wallet.

A nurse came up to the woman, and they exchanged a few words.

"Give your card to this young man," the woman said. "He can finish the paperwork. The nurse will take you back."

David took Frank's wallet from his shaking hand. "I'll handle the rest of this admission stuff and stay with the kids," David said, gesturing toward Loretta's children. "Don't worry, Frank."

Frank addressed his stepchildren. "Everything's going to be fine. I'll come out with news as soon as I can. David will be with you. If you need anything, ask him." He turned to the nurse, who was gesturing to him to follow her. The two set off into the interior of the hospital at a brisk pace.

...from **When Dreams There Be**

ALSO BY BARBARA HINSKE

Available at Amazon in Print, Audio, and for Kindle

The Rosemont Series

Coming to Rosemont

Weaving the Strands

Uncovering Secrets

Drawing Close

Bringing Them Home

Shelving Doubts

Restoring What Was Lost

No Matter How Far

When Dreams There Be

Novellas

The Night Train

The Christmas Club (adapted

for The Hallmark Channel, 2019)

Paws & Pastries

Sweets & Treats

Snowflakes, Cupcakes & Kittens

Workout Wishes & Valentine Kisses

Wishes of Home

Novels in the Guiding Emily Series

Guiding Emily

The Unexpected Path

Over Every Hurdle

Down the Aisle

Novels in the "Who's There?!" Collection

Deadly Parcel

Final Circuit

Connect with BARBARA HINSKE Online
Sign up for her newsletter at **BarbaraHinske.com**
Goodreads.com/BarbaraHinske
Facebook.com/BHinske
Instagram/barbarahinskeauthor
TikTok.com/BarbaraHinske
Pinterest.com/BarbaraHinske
Twitter.com/BarbaraHinske
Search for **Barbara Hinske on YouTube**
bhinske@gmail.com

Made in the USA
Monee, IL
06 February 2025

11639272R00083